SPIRIT HUNTERS

THE ISLAND OF MONSTERS

ELLEN OH

SPIRIT HUNTERS

THE ISLAND OF MONSTERS

HARPER

An Imprint of HarperCollins*Publishers*

Library of Congress Control Number: 2017956220
ISBN 978-0-06-243011-3

Typography by Andrea Vandergrift
18 19 20 21 22   CG/LSCH   10 9 8 7 6 5 4 3 2 1
❖
First Edition

This book is dedicated to all the monsters that keep us up all night, too afraid to go to the bathroom.

SPIRIT HUNTERS

THE ISLAND OF MONSTERS

MISSING GHOSTS
Tuesday, October 3

Our Lady of Mercy's cemetery was the last place most people would want to be after dark, but tonight Harper Raine wove her way through the headstones, seeking out the dead. In her hands, she carried a plastic container filled with the black spiritual residue of a vanquished evil spirit. It was why she was there so late on a school night.

Except she couldn't just dump it anywhere. The residents took issue with where you dumped evil residue.

Harper looked up at the darkening sky and cursed. One of the things she hated the most about autumn was how quickly the sun set. They were only in the first week of October, and it was already dusk by six thirty p.m.

Normally Our Lady of Mercy was not a scary graveyard. It was a really pretty place, with well-tended old graves. No new ones. Most of the headstones were over fifty years old. But the spreading darkness cast everything into shadows that seemed to hide dangers around each corner. Even more disturbing was the atmosphere. For the first time, Harper felt uneasy.

Suddenly, a figure with bright-red hair popped up in front of her.

"Where is everyone?" her oldest friend, Rose, asked. "I just went down to visit Mrs. Taylor under the willow tree, and she's not there."

Slightly alarmed, Harper headed toward the willow tree, the last of the sun's setting rays gleaming through its delicate leaves as dusk ended and night fell.

"Are you sure she isn't anywhere?" Harper asked. She walked in a big circle around the tree. Mrs. Taylor always knew the best places for Harper to drop off spiritual residue. Stopping at a large headstone, Harper knelt on the ground and pressed her hand on top of the grave. She sensed nothing. Harper was disturbed. Mrs. Taylor was her favorite at the cemetery. She was very motherly and had been a loving presence for many of the young ghosts. Harper couldn't imagine Our Lady of Mercy without Mrs. Taylor and her perpetual knitting.

Darkness closed in on them in one fell swoop. Harper immediately regretted her decision to come to the graveyard. "We're going to have to leave soon or I'll be in big trouble."

A sudden noise from behind caused her to jump.

"Harper! I'm so glad you're here! I need to talk to you!" The ghostly form of a young teenage boy appeared before her eyes. He was dark haired and wore a leather jacket over his ratty jeans.

"Hi, Roderick," Harper said, in relief. "Do you know where everyone is? We can't find Mrs. Taylor."

Roderick was quiet; he seemed distracted and not himself. "That's the strangest thing," he said. "I think I'm the only one around."

At his words, Rose began to flicker. "That's impossible! There are thirty spirits in this place, and they are bound to their bodies. They can't all leave the cemetery!"

"Don't you think I know that?" Roderick snapped, his bluish aura glowing bright with his emotions. "The other day they were here with me, and now they're gone. Everyone!"

The ghost boy faded again, looking unsure of himself for the first time since Harper had met him earlier in the summer. "I don't get it. Why'd they leave me behind?"

Disturbed, Harper shared an uneasy glance with Rose.

"Can you tell us what's happened?" Harper said.

The ghost whirled around and drifted away. "I remember it was a few nights ago. Phoebe was upset because she thought the twins were hiding from her. But we looked everywhere, and we didn't sees no signs of them. Then the next night, we noticed that Mary Lou and Mr. Garvey were gone."

"Mr. Garvey?" Harper asked.

"Yeah, you know—the old guy with the cane who always yells?"

Harper nodded.

"Then some more folks just up and vanished, and then the old lady under the willow tree who's always knitting nothing, Mrs. Taylor. Phoebe was real broken up about that. You know she was like a grandma to her."

Harper smiled at the "knitting nothing" comment. It was true that Mrs. Taylor's knitting never amounted to anything. After all, she was a ghost. But she had told Harper once that just the motions of knitting were so soothing that she could not stop.

Roderick looked upset. "It's not funny, Harper."

"Oh no, I wasn't laughing about the situation, I was just thinking about . . . never mind. Go on."

"Every night Phoebe and I would come out and sees more of them is missing, until tonight Phoebe's gone, too," he said. He hung in the air, turning in a slow circle as if still looking for his missing friends. "I'm the only one left."

This upset Harper. She remembered the first time she met all the cemetery ghosts earlier this summer. Her family had just moved to Washington, D.C., from New York City, right into a haunted house. When the evil ghost had possessed her brother, Michael, Harper had been desperate for help. She'd come to this cemetery to seek a spiritual adviser. And it was the ghosts who'd helped her. For that, she would always be grateful to them.

"Do you remember anything strange? Did somebody come through? Did you feel anything weird?" Harper asked.

He shook his head slowly. "I didn't feel nothing. First they was here, and then they wasn't. If they was all going somewhere, then why didn't they take me with them?" Roderick looked sad and confused.

"I doubt they'd leave you, Rod," Rose said.

"Something's happening here. We'll have to look into it, right, Harper?"

Harper was already walking past the willow tree toward the graves at the back of the cemetery. Rose and Roderick floated after her.

"You said the twins were first?" Harper asked. She pulled out a small flashlight and shone it on the headstones, searching through the names.

"Yeah, they're over in the corner," Roderick said as he flew ahead to show her the way. He alighted on an elaborate headstone covered in sculpted roses. It was one of the farthest graves from the church, fenced in by ornate wrought iron gates that bordered the public park.

Harper knelt at their grave, trying to feel for spiritual emanations but coming up empty.

Turning slowly to survey the cemetery, Harper noticed the pattern of disappearances. "First the twins, Mr. Garvey, and Mary Lou." She followed the headstones back, noticing that Roderick was the closest to the church. He'd always complained about the fact that he was the only one stuck all alone and away from the others. None of the graves around him were haunted. "Roderick, whatever you do, don't wander far from your grave tonight!"

"But if my friends are in trouble, shouldn't I be

trying to help them?" he asked.

Harper shook her head. "You don't know what you're dealing with. You need to be careful. I'll come back as soon as I have some answers." She looked anxiously at the dark sky and started heading for the front gate. Her mother hated it when she rode her bike in the dark.

"Hey, guys, do you have to leave so soon?" Roderick asked in a plaintive voice.

"I've got to go home or my parents are going to ground me," Harper said.

Rose materialized suddenly in front of her. "But what about Roderick? We can't leave him alone!"

Harper skidded to a halt, not wanting to walk through her friend. "We can come back tomorrow after school, but I have to go now or I won't be able to do anything," Harper said. She sidestepped around her friend and out the gates into the church drive-way, where she'd left her bike. Looking back, she saw Roderick drooping despondently by the entranceway. "Rod, promise me you'll stay put, and don't go after anything new or strange, okay?" The dark-haired ghost nodded.

"I'll see you tomorrow," Harper said. She strapped on her helmet and started down the road. Rose half floated, half sat curled up in the basket, facing her.

"You're forgetting something," Rose said, pointing to the plastic container Harper had put back into the bottom of her basket.

"Crud!" Harper snatched up the container and sped back into the graveyard. The only reason she'd come all the way to the church was to get rid of the residue. She should have just gone home after vanquishing the evil spirit, but the idea of having spirit gunk in her room all night had creeped her out. She had an irrational fear of what was essentially the remains of a ghost. A ghost that had been troubling a playground full of little kids.

With a quick apology to Roderick, she dumped the residue in a spot between the graves and the side of the church. Opening her black messenger bag, she pulled out a bottle labeled "Holy Water" and rinsed her container thoroughly before throwing everything back into her bag. She raced to her bike and sped away.

"You should fill up on holy water before we go," Rose said.

"Can't," Harper responded. "Don't have time."

Rose looked at her with disapproval. "You are down to one bottle, Harper. That's not safe. Your grandma always said to stock up. And you wouldn't be so low if you hadn't insisted on doing that exorcism

8

alone today. You almost got yourself killed! You're just lucky that Dayo showed up when she did and distracted that ghost."

Harper scrunched up her face in annoyance. Rose was right. If Dayo hadn't shown up, Harper would've been in big trouble. The ghost had been smart and had tricked Harper into breaking her salt circle. Dayo had arrived in time to save Harper from getting her head smashed by a swing. Together they'd been able to defeat the ghost, just like earlier that summer when Dayo helped Harper fight the ghosts that were possessing her brother. The best thing that had happened to Harper since moving to Washington, D.C., was becoming friends with Dayo.

"I had to do something about it. That nasty ghost pushed Jacob off the swing and broke his arm!" Jacob was her little brother's friend.

There was something very unsettling about receiving a glare of disapproval from a ghost, for Rose's spiritual aura glowed darker with her emotions.

"You should have waited for your grandmother or taken Dayo with you in the first place," Rose said.

Harper sighed. Even though Rose was three years older, she usually didn't lecture Harper. But Rose was right. Harper shouldn't have done the exorcism by herself. She should have waited for her grandmother, a shaman and premiere spirit hunter, to come home from her trip. Knowing her friend was right irritated Harper even more.

Rose had been Harper's best friend since she was four years old. She'd been craving the chocolate that her mother had left in a candy bowl in front of the foyer mirror. When no one was looking, Harper climbed up onto the table to steal some chocolate. But all thoughts of candy flew out of her head when she found a pretty girl with bright curly red hair and light blue eyes waving hello. They'd been best friends ever since.

"I'm really worried. What if something happens to Roderick?" Rose asked.

Harper winced. She'd almost forgotten about the ghost boy. He was so unlike his usual mischievous self. The first time Harper met Roderick, he'd been gently teasing the ghost girl Phoebe and joking about putting a spider down Harper's back, which was not cool. It was hard to see him so sad and distraught.

"I'm going to call Grandma as soon as we get home and tell her all about it." Disappearing ghosts was something even Harper knew was out of her league.

"But she's not home until next week! He might be gone tonight."

Harper kept pedaling faster, praying that she'd beat her parents home. It was already seven o'clock, and recently they'd been getting home by seven thirty. It would be a close call.

"Harper, are you listening to me?" Rose asked, rearing up from the basket into Harper's face.

"Gah! Don't do that!" Harper nearly crashed her bicycle but was able to right herself at the last moment. "I heard you! I promise, we'll go back tomorrow and see what we can do. But Rose, if I get grounded, there's nothing I can do to help."

The ghost girl sat back with a sigh. "I know, you're right," she said. "But I have such a bad feeling about this. Don't you?"

"Yeah," Harper agreed. "It was weird and creepy. How can thirty ghosts simply vanish all at the same time? But I'm sure Grandma will know what to do. Don't worry about Roderick—we'll come back tomorrow."

Rose nodded, her red curls billowing all around her. "Yes, she'll know. She must."

IN TROUBLE AGAIN
Tuesday, October 3—Evening

Unfortunately, by the time Harper pulled into her driveway, she could see both cars already parked, and her heart sank. She opened the garage door and left her bicycle and helmet on the ground before running inside.

She walked into the dining room to find her family eating without her.

"Wash up and sit down," her mother said with a stern glance.

Her father gave her a disappointed stare, while her older sister, Kelly, didn't even bother to look up from her plate. Only Michael seemed happy to see her, waving his chopsticks enthusiastically in the air.

She gave him a little wave and ran to the bathroom to wash up. Rose appeared next to her.

"They look real mad," she said.

Harper sighed. "What else is new," she said.

"I'll wait for you upstairs," Rose said. "Good luck!"

Harper was envious of her friend's ability to hide from her parents. She dragged her feet as she went to sit down in her seat next to Michael. Her father passed her a paper plate, and she began to help herself to the Chinese food still in takeout containers set on the table. Hunger pangs hit hard as she filled her plate with beef chow fun noodles, salt-and-pepper squid, fried tofu in gravy, and steamed dumplings. She immediately started shoving big bites into her mouth.

"Harper, your manners, please," her mother said, cutting off Kelly's endless prattle about her day at school and her friends and her lack of a boyfriend. "Before we talk about where you were, we need to discuss logistics for our trip this month."

Kelly squealed with delight. "I can't believe we're going to the Caribbean for Halloween! All my friends are so jealous! I'll be the only one with a tan!"

"Tanning is bad for you," Harper said. "It'll give you skin cancer."

Kelly shrugged. "That's what sunscreen is for."

"I don't wanna go!" Michael pouted. He'd asked for an Iron Man costume for Halloween. "I wanna go trick-or-treating with my friends."

"If we stay with Grandma, then I could take him trick-or-treating," Harper offered up quickly.

Her mother gave Harper the look, and Harper sank down into her seat. She hated that look. It was her mother's warning that said she was about to go too far. And yet, even knowing she was in danger, Harper couldn't help herself.

"Grandma would love to have us . . ."

Yuna Raine put her chopsticks down carefully and folded her hands together over her plate.

"Harper, how many times must we have this conversation? Our entire family is going on this vacation, whether you like it or not. I don't want to have this discussion again. Are we clear?"

Harper gave a sullen nod and shoved an entire dumpling into her mouth as her parents began to discuss the logistics for the trip. They were all going to miss a few days of school, which was usually a big no-no in the Raine family. Except that this vacation was set up at the insistence of her uncle Justin and aunt Caroline Richmond. Aunt Caroline was her father's younger sister and a hotel manager for the

Bennington Hotel chain. She'd been sent to over-see the grand reopening of the Grande Bennington Hotel Resort and Beach Club at Razu Island, and her uncle Justin was made head pastry chef at the same location. The grand reopening was set for the end of October and would culminate with a huge party on Halloween night. Kelly had been planning her costume for weeks, ever since first hearing about the trip. But Harper was dreading the ordeal. Her grand-mother had already warned her that Rose would not be able to make the long trip. Although the ghost girl could travel with Harper in a compact mirror, she could not be away from her original medium, the decorative mirror that hung in the foyer, for too long. Harper had recently been reunited with Rose. She didn't want to be apart from her, not even if it was for a nice vacation.

Michael nudged her arm. "Where's Rose?" he whispered.

Harper pointed at the ceiling, which satisfied Michael.

"I saw a ghost cat today," he whispered. "It looked sad and lost."

"Probably happened recently, then," Harper explained. "Did it bother you?"

He stuffed more food into his mouth before

shaking his head. "It runned away."

"You mean ran away," Harper said.

"That's what I said, it runned away," Michael insisted.

She reached over and ruffled his hair, even though he hated it. There was nobody in the world she loved more than her baby brother. After the horrible ghost-possession incident, Harper was more protective of Michael than ever.

As they finished up their meal, her mother gave her a serious look. "Do you mind telling me where you were tonight?"

"I was just biking around, and I lost track of time," Harper said.

"Was Dayo with you?" her mother asked hopefully.

Harper shook her head.

"Tell me the truth—were you visiting a cemetery again?" Yuna asked.

Harper bit her lip and nodded. Her mother and father had been told about her junior shaman status by her grandma Lee, but they didn't approve. The truth was, they really didn't believe in ghosts. But too many things that couldn't be explained had happened to their family, and it had become impossible for them to ignore the possibility of the supernatural.

However, their mode of acceptance was to not talk about it. Ever. Even Michael had learned to keep quiet about his encounters with the spirit world. Neither of her lawyerly parents wanted to accept the fact that two of their children could talk to ghosts. And Kelly, who'd also suffered through the worst of Michael's possession, remained intentionally unaware of the spiritual world. At least, that was what it looked like to Harper. Whenever she asked Kelly about the events that had happened earlier that summer, Kelly would categorically deny that anything weird had happened. She even claimed that the attack, when Michael smashed a toy fire truck in her face while he was possessed by the evil ghost, was just an accident. Even with the faint scar on her forehead, Kelly refused to listen to what had really happened. Harper had taken to calling her Cleopatra, Queen of Denial.

A look of worry mixed with disappointment crossed her mother's face. Harper hated that look. "Well, you know the rule. No riding your bike after dark by yourself. Since we can't trust you to follow that rule, you are grounded for a week. Pick up Michael after school, and come straight home."

When Harper began to protest, her mother held up a hand to stop her. "Not a word, Harper, or I'll make it until we leave for our trip."

Harper clammed up right away. She couldn't risk being grounded for nearly three weeks.

After a drawn-out silence, her mother excused Harper from the table. Harper pushed her chair back and stomped up the stairs.

Once in her room, Harper threw herself onto her bed and fumed into her pillow.

"What happened?" Rose asked, materializing next to her.

"I'm grounded for a week!"

"Oh no! What about Roderick?! How are we going to help him?"

"Aw, shoot!" Harper sat up. Grabbing the phone, she called her grandmother's cell phone. When it went straight into voice mail, she flipped open her laptop and began to compose an email.

"What are you doing?" Rose asked.

"Grandma never checks her voice mail," Harper said. "But she does check email. I'm letting her know what's happened and asking her to look into it."

Rose was wringing her hands as she floated around the room. "But what if Roderick disappears, too? We have to do something to help him!"

"There's nothing I can do," Harper said.

"We can go right after school and check on him then," Rose cut in.

"I'm grounded!"

"So what? That's never stopped you before!"

"Kelly will definitely rat me out if I leave her with Michael again," Harper said. "I can't risk it."

"You have to! Roderick is a friend of ours!"

"Then you go check on him!" Harper snapped, tired of the conversation.

"Fine! I will!" Rose yelled back as she disappeared.

Harper regretted her words immediately. "Rose, come back," she said. "I didn't mean it. I'm sorry."

A few minutes passed before she heard Rose's voice again. "It's all right. I know you're cranky 'cause of your mom. But I think I need to go and see what's happening over there."

The thought of Rose going out by herself filled Harper with fear. "No, Rose! If something happened to you, I would never forgive myself!"

The ghost girl reappeared, this time within the reflection of the ornate mirror on Harper's bureau. "Don't worry about me. I can take care of myself." Rose smiled at her. "I'm going to go tonight and report back to you in the morning, okay?"

She flew out of the mirror to give Harper a ghostly hug. "Hey, don't look so scared! I promise I'll be here before you wake up. You know you'd never get up in time if it wasn't for me."

With one last hug, Rose disappeared, leaving Harper with a sudden intense, eerie fright, which sat in the pit of her stomach. She couldn't help but fear that Rose was in over her head.

WHERE'S ROSE?
Wednesday, October 4

The next morning, Harper woke to the sound of her alarm clock. For the first time ever, she was wide awake without having to hit snooze ten times. She sat up in bed, looking around in confusion.

"Rose? Are you here?"

There was no answer. The dread that had been sitting in her stomach since last night had now grown to a sizable knot. She knew something bad had happened to Rose. It wasn't like her to break a promise. Something had happened at the cemetery. Something that had kept Rose from coming home.

Harper got ready for school quickly and raced downstairs. Her mother was drinking coffee and

Michael was eating a toaster waffle. Her father must have already left for work and taken Kelly to school. Her parents were both big-time attorneys at a large law firm in downtown D.C., but they didn't always carpool together, which Harper thought was a terrible crime against the environment.

"Harper!" Michael beamed at her, his face covered with maple syrup and milk.

"Hey, buddy," Harper said. She grabbed a waffle from the toaster, even though she wasn't hungry. She didn't want another lecture from her mother. Sitting down, she tried to think of how she could go over to the church without getting in trouble.

"You want me to give you a lift to school, honey?" her mother asked.

"No thanks, I'm gonna ride my bike," Harper replied.

Her mother gave her a sharp look. "You're picking up Michael after school. I don't want you riding with him in the basket again, Harper. That's incredibly dangerous."

"I won't. I'll walk with him, don't worry." Harper sighed. "Mom, I know I'm grounded, but I need to go to the library to do a project. If I'm home before five, can I go?"

"You can go, but you have to take Michael with you," her mother said.

"But, Mom!"

"He'll sit quietly and read," she said. "And I want you to come straight home afterward, okay?"

The set look on her mother's face told Harper this was a no-win argument. "Yes, Mom."

Michael had started whooping with joy at the idea of going out to the library.

"Harper, can we take out a lot of books this time? Like fifty or a hundred?"

"That might be too heavy for your sister," their mother cut in. "Why don't you just grab two or three for now, okay, honey?"

Harper played with her waffle, barely eating it. All her thoughts were centered around Rose and getting over to the cemetery.

"Don't you need to get going?"

With another long sigh, Harper grabbed her school bag and started to head out the door.

"Harper?" her mother called to her.

She stopped at the kitchen door to look at her mother impatiently.

"If you would just be a little more positive about this trip, I know you would have a good time, okay?"

With an indifferent nod, Harper took off.

At the corner, Harper saw her other best friend, Dayo, waiting for her. They became the best of friends from the moment they met earlier that summer. There was nothing quite like surviving a dangerous exorcism to cement a friendship for life.

Dayo's smiling face grew serious as she saw Harper's grim expression.

"What's up?" Dayo asked.

"Rose is gone," Harper replied as she launched into everything that had happened the night before.

"Oh Harper, this is terrible!" Dayo said. "What are we going to do?"

"I need to go to the church to check out what's happened, but my mom grounded me and I have to watch Michael," Harper said. "And since Michael can't ride in the basket, there's no way I can go with him."

"I'll watch him at my house," Dayo offered.

Harper's relief was intense. "Thanks, Dayo. You're the best."

"I know," Dayo said. "But don't you forget it."

After what felt like the longest day of school, Harper and Dayo rode over to the elementary school to pick up Michael.

"You okay, Harper?" Dayo asked.

Harper sighed. "I feel like I just got Rose back, and now I've lost her again."

Dayo patted Harper on the shoulder consolingly.

The doors flung open and a crowd of kindergartners peered out, looking for their parents. Harper bolted forward to let the teacher know she was there.

"That's my sister!" Michael yelled.

The other kindergartners waved and shouted hello. Michael jumped into Harper's arms with a squeal of delight.

"Argh, you're getting so big and heavy!" Harper groused.

"I know! I'm a big boy now!" Michael said as he slipped down and grabbed Harper's hand. "Hi Dayo! Can we stop by your house for your mom's cookies?"

"Michael, you can't invite yourself over like that!"

Dayo laughed. "Well, that's what I was going to do! My mom is probably baking cookies and will need some taste testers." Dayo's mother was an amazing chef and ran her own catering business.

"Oh boy, that rocks!" Michael said as he beamed up at them.

This sent the girls into a fit of laughter, and they got their bikes and walked the six blocks to Dayo's home. Harper gave Mrs. Clayton a hug and took two of her famous white chocolate–cranberry cookies before heading to the cemetery.

When she got there, she ran straight over to Roderick's grave.

"Roderick, are you there?" Harper called. "Roderick! Can you hear me?"

She placed her hands on the grave and closed her eyes, but she felt nothing. Roderick was gone.

"He's dead—he can't hear you," a voice said from behind her.

She whirled around and stared into the face of the old church caretaker.

"Little girl, I always see you here talking with the gravestones, and I don't think nothing much of it. Different strokes and all. But I gotta think this just ain't healthy for a young girl like you. You should be hanging out with your friends and leaving the dead alone," the caretaker said.

He walked away, muttering under his breath about weird kids these days. Harper paid no attention to him. She sat down on Roderick's grave and wrapped her arms around her knees. No matter how much she opened her mind, she could feel no spiritual energy anywhere in the graveyard. It was entirely empty of any ghosts. Where were they? How could they possibly have all been pulled away from their resting places? She didn't even know where to look or what to look for.

She knew in her heart that Rose was in trouble. But there was nothing she could do to help her oldest friend. She wiped away the tears that had seeped from under her lids. There was only one person who could help.

She needed her grandmother.

GRANDMA LEE'S HOUSE
Friday, October 6

It wasn't until Friday afternoon that Harper finally heard the news she was waiting for. Her grandmother sent her a brief email that said she was home and resting after a difficult spiritual intervention.

Relieved, Harper ran downstairs to look for Michael. Opening the basement door, she heard the sound of violent cartoons playing from the family room. She felt guilty about ignoring her little brother all afternoon.

"Michael!" Harper yelled. "Do you want to go to Grandma's house for dinner?"

She heard a muffled whoop of glee and then the thudding of running feet as Michael's little frame rushed into view. She braced herself as he flung his body onto her legs, hugging her hard.

"How did you know I wanted to go? Did you read my mind? I was hoping and hoping, but I didn't want to bug you," he said in a rush.

Harper leaned down to kiss her brother's grubby face. The orange remnants of Cheetos dotted his chin and the corners of his lips.

"But how we gonna go, Harper?" Michael asked. "You aren't allowed to take me in your basket anymore."

"No problem," Harper said.

She picked up her cell phone and called her mom.

"Harper, is everything okay?" Yuna said as soon as she answered.

"Yeah, Michael and I are bored. Dayo is busy with family, and we have nothing to do."

"Can't Kelly take you out?"

"She's going to a rally at her school," Harper said. "She's not gonna want to do anything with us instead."

"Well, have her take you to the rally. It sounds like fun."

"Grandma's home also. Maybe she could drop us off there?"

Yuna hesitated before responding. "Only if she's

willing to—it would be out of the way for her."

"Okay, I'll ask. Thanks, Mom."

Harper then motioned Michael to follow her upstairs to Kelly's room. She knocked on the door and then poked her head in. Her sister was absorbed in the act of painting her toenails.

"Get out," Kelly said.

Ignoring her, Harper asked, "Hey Kelly, didn't you say there's some rally up at school tonight?"

"Uh-huh. Now get out," Kelly replied, not lifting her head up from her careful examination of her big toe.

"Well, Mom said that you need to take us with you," Harper said.

"What? I'm not babysitting you two all night! Why can't you guys just stay home? I was gonna order you some pizza before I left."

Harper shrugged. "I don't want to. Mom's forcing us to go out, and you have to take us."

"That's it! I'm calling Mom!"

"I tried," Harper said. "It's no use. You know how she gets. 'It's a Friday night—you should go do something fun with Michael,' blah, blah, blah. And she and Dad are working on a big case together and won't be home until late."

Kelly slammed her fist on her desk. "It's 'cause you are a freak with no friends!"

"Hey!" Michael shouted. "That's mean! Dayo's her friend! And mine."

The insult didn't faze Harper at all. She was used to Kelly's temper. But she grinned at Michael's righteous indignation on her behalf.

"Look," Harper cut in, holding Michael back from attacking Kelly. "It's not like we want to hang out with you all night, either. We'd rather be at Grandma's than at a stupid rally."

Harper could see the thought process occurring in Kelly's brain before she even spoke.

"So, Grandma's back?" Kelly asked nonchalantly.

"Yep."

"Would you rather I dropped you off at Grandma's and picked you up after the rally?"

"I don't know—what do you say, Michael?" Harper asked.

"Yeah, at Grandma's!" Michael shouted. He turned around and clapped his hand over his mouth to stifle his giggle.

"Fine, then," Kelly sighed. "I'll drop you off on my way, but you guys better not make me late! Get out!" She shooed them out and slammed the door.

They heard the loud click of the lock.

Harper and Michael grinned and high-fived each other.

"So, does Grandma know we're coming?" Michael asked.

"No, I thought we'd try to surprise her," Harper responded.

"Oh goody! We never get to surprise her."

An hour later Kelly turned into the driveway of their grandma's little house in the suburbs of Maryland.

"Tell Grandma I can't stop right now. But I'll come in when I pick you guys up, okay?" Kelly said.

"All right, thanks, Kelly!" Harper said. She and Michael jumped out and waved good-bye before heading up the driveway. The front door opened, and they could see their grandmother smiling at them, her little Yorkie spinning in circles from excitement.

"Good timing! Dinner is ready," Grandma said with a beaming smile.

"Grandma!" Michael cried out as he rushed in and tackled the small form of their grandmother. "How'd you know we were coming? Did the ghosts tell you again?"

Grandma laughed as she bear-hugged him. "How many times do I have to tell you? I can't share all my secrets!" Releasing him, she reached over to accept Harper's hug.

"And why didn't Kelly stop by? She's too busy for her old grandma?"

Harper shook her head. "She was running late to her school thing. She'll stop by later."

"Wait, wait!" Grandma Lee grabbed Michael by the back of his shirt as he made to run into the living room, chasing after Monty. "Shoes off!"

The homey kitchen table was set with three place settings, bowls of rice, and an assortment of the little side dishes that made Korean food so tasty. Harper and Michael were only half Korean, but it was their favorite cuisine. Unfortunately, they didn't get to eat it often. Only at their grandmother's house did they get a real home-cooked meal. Both their parents were too busy to cook, and when they did, it would usually be Italian or American, or frozen pizza.

With a happy sigh, Harper sat down as her grandmother brought over steaming-hot bowls of spicy pork stew. She watched as Michael picked up pieces of *kim*, salty roasted seaweed, and maneuvered them onto hot clumps of rice. He shoved them into his mouth, chased down by bunches of tiny sautéed anchovies and pickled cabbage. The little Yorkie sat at his feet, hoping he'd drop some food.

"So, what brings two of my favorite grandchildren to visit?" Grandma said as she picked up her chopsticks.

Michael giggled. "Grandma, you only have three!"

"Not much longer," Harper said. "Auntie Youjin is having her baby soon, right?" Auntie Youjin was their mother's younger sister, an investment banker who was expecting her first child.

Their grandmother nodded. "She says she will have a C-section in November. But I know the baby will come before Halloween. So, I'll take the bus up to New York before then."

"Whassa C-section?" Michael asked.

"It's when they cut open the mommy's stomach to take the baby out," Grandma said.

"EEEEWWWWW! Yuck!" Michael made a face and then laughed.

Harper shot her grandmother a reproachful look. "Now he'll be telling all his friends that babies get cut out of their mommies' bellies."

"So, what's the problem with that? Better than saying you push the baby out just like you would push poo-poo," she said.

"Grandma!" Harper shouted as Michael shrieked with laughter, chortling so hard food was spilling down his chin. Grandma wiped him up and told him to shush.

"Why is your sister in such a bad mood?" she asked the giggling boy.

Michael swallowed before answering. "I think it's because of Rose," he whispered. "I haven't seen her around the house at all. But Harper wouldn't tell me nothing."

"Oh? The ghost girl from the mirror?" Grandma asked. "What happened?"

"Grandma, why do you even have email if you never read them?" Harper asked in exasperation. "I wrote to tell you that Rose has been missing for several days!" Her voice trembled a little at her pronouncement.

Grandma frowned. "My eyes aren't too good at reading the computer screen. That's why I just emailed you to tell you I was home, so that we can talk in person."

"You don't even listen to your voice mail," Harper complained.

Her grandmother waved a hand. "Too complicated!"

"I don't even know why you bother to have a phone, then!"

"Because at least it tells me you called," her grandmother responded. "Do you know where Rose went? Even though I unbound her from the mirror, she can't travel too far or stay away too long—otherwise she'll weaken and be unable to return."

Harper quickly explained all that had happened, and a stab of fear caused her to wince. She couldn't imagine being without Rose.

When Rose was fifteen, she was diagnosed with tuberculosis. It was a slow and deadly disease at the time due to lack of good medical care. Because the light hurt Rose's eyes, her mother blocked out all the light in her room with heavy curtains. She also never opened any windows, thinking the air was dangerous. So, Rose became a prisoner in her own room. When Rose had a good day, her mother would sit her in front of her vanity mirror, brushing her hair, telling her how beautiful she was, how she couldn't live without her. And when Rose died, her spirit became stuck in that heavy, grief-stricken room. With no light for her to follow, Rose found herself floating into the mirror, where the flickering lights of the candles shone the brightest. Once inside the mirror, she became trapped, until the fateful day when she met Harper.

It was only after moving to Washington, D.C.,

that Harper learned that her Grandma Lee was a spirit hunter. Harper asked her to help Rose become free of her mirror.

Grandma Lee had performed a shamanistic ritual that had released Rose's spirit from the mirror for short periods of time so that she could move through anything with a reflection. That was why Harper could carry Rose in a compact mirror wherever she went. Rose loved her freedom and would sometimes go away for several hours by herself.

But this was the first time ever that the ghost girl had been gone for so long.

"I'll ask Mrs. Devereux to go find her for you," Grandma said.

Harper felt some of her tension drain away. If anyone could find her, it would be the greatest of Grandma's spiritual guides, Mrs. Devereux.

GOOD-BYE, OLD FRIEND
Saturday, October 7

Saturday afternoon, Yuna took Michael to his swim lessons at the local YMCA, Kelly was out with friends, and Harper was sitting in front of her house feeling bored. Dayo had to babysit her cousin for her aunt, and Harper had nothing to do. Just as she thought about calling her grandmother, a big white Cadillac pulled up, honking its horn.

"Harper, go get your bag. We have to go," Grandma Lee shouted. She was all decked out in her red-and-white shaman robes with gold patterning on the shoulders and on the hem of her long, full silk skirt.

Harper ran into the house and headed to her

room to grab her black messenger bag. Opening it, she checked to see that her two shaman bells, Wisdom and Truth, and her *mudang* bells, with the long metal handle split into two dragon heads, each holding a ring of six tiger bells from its mouth, were strapped inside and covered by a fine netting that kept them from ringing while in her bag. She also made sure her three shallow brass bowls were there, as well as a full bottle of holy water and a large container of sea salt. Satisfied, she closed up her bag and headed outside.

"I know what happened to Rose," Grandma Lee said, a grim look on her usually smiling face. "Can we go pick up Dayo also? We're going to need all the help we can get."

"Dayo's busy. Do you want to wait until she's free?"

Grandma Lee shook her head. "No, we have to move quickly before we lose it."

"Lose what?" Harper asked.

"The creature who took Rose."

Stunned by her grandmother's disclosure, Harper got silently into the car.

They arrived at an old house that was not too far from Our Lady of Mercy. All the curtains were drawn, and the house itself seemed to pulse with a dark energy. As they parked, a few women rushed over from the house next door, bowing and crying in relief.

"Thank you for coming, Mrs. Lee," the oldest of the women said in Korean. "We can take your granddaughter next door and give her something delicious to eat."

"My granddaughter is going to help me," Grandma Lee replied in English.

The women looked surprised but nodded in agreement. As Harper and Grandma Lee approached the haunted house, the old women hung back. Harper didn't blame them. A strong negative energy pulsed from the house, like a physical assault. And then Harper felt a rush of spiritual energy so intense that she had to close off her senses to keep it from overwhelming her.

"They don't want us here," Harper said.

"Too bad," Grandma retorted. "It's not wanted here, either!"

"What happened, Grandma?"

"It's very strange. When you told me about the missing ghosts in the graveyard, I immediately thought it could be a soul eater, a rare type of evil creature that gains power from capturing lost souls. I've never actually seen one before, only heard of them."

Grandma paused and turned to look at Harper. "And then I heard about this house. Something evil moved into it last week. The family fled the house in fear, and even the neighbors are terribly frightened. When they called me in to check it out, I immediately noticed the incredible levels of spiritual emanations that are coming from here. I realized that this is where all the missing ghosts must be."

Harper was alarmed. "Rose! Is she in there?" Harper made to rush into the house, but her grandmother quickly held her back.

"You must be careful," she said. "This thing doesn't just hunt spirits, it devours them for energy. You must keep your bells close to you at all times. It is the only thing that can keep you safe."

Without hesitation, Harper grabbed hold of Wisdom tightly in her hand. The Wisdom bell was also called the Ancient One, and it began and ended every exorcism.

Grandma Lee pulled out her *mudang* bells from her bag. She began to shake them before her as she entered the house, leaving Harper to follow in her wake.

Inside, it was dark. Only a few strands of light shone through the curtains. Harper flipped the light switch on, only to see it turned off a second later.

When she turned the light on again, the light bulbs shattered. The stench of sulfur and electricity was so strong that Harper could taste it on her tongue.

"Oh boy, they really don't want us here," she said.

"They never do," Grandma said.

In the living room, they set up their bowls and bells quickly in a large circle and then filled all the bowls with holy water. Around the outside of the circle, Grandma Lee poured a thick border of sea salt. Sitting back-to-back, they sat in a salt-enclosed circle of six bowls and four bells. Then Grandma Lee steadily rang her *mudang* bells.

The floor under them rumbled, and the house creaked as if someone was trying to pull the beams apart.

"Harper, no matter what happens, don't leave the circle," her grandmother said.

Harper nodded, shivering. The temperature in the house had dropped dramatically. She could see her breath frosting before her. The water in her bowls froze over, and icicles formed above her head, sharp and jagged. The smell of burning electrical wires made Harper's eyes water.

"Remember, it's just an illusion," Grandma assured her. "It's just like all those times before. It cannot harm you unless you believe it."

Insects crawled out from under the furniture and down the walls, blanketing the floor in a massive black wave of movement. The wave surged toward them, only to halt at the salt border.

"When do we begin the binding chant?" Harper asked.

"Not yet," Grandma said. "It's not close enough."

The insects were climbing on top of each other, forming a high wall. They were beginning to drop over the salt and toward Harper.

"Grandma!" Panic was threatening to overwhelm her.

"Use Truth!" her grandmother shouted.

Harper rang the Truth bell hard, sending the sea of insects crashing back into nothingness.

There came a ghastly sound unlike anything that Harper had ever heard in her entire life. Her flesh was riddled with goose bumps, and the back of her neck was tingling with the awareness of something frightening and close. An unclean stench caused Harper to gag in disgust.

"Sacrifice . . ."

The sibilant voice was soft and whispery yet absolutely clear. The voice entered into her head and grew louder and sharper, piercing her eardrums.

Grandma Lee rang her binder bell, a medium-toned sound that broke through the agony inflicted by the evil spirit's voice. A scream of sheer rage filled the house, and then, right in front of Harper, there stood a soul eater.

It had pale white leather-like skin and a skeletal frame at odds with its abnormally distended belly. Its unnaturally long limbs and fingers and the strange way it held its body reminded Harper of a praying mantis. But it was its face that was most disturbing. Over a large red slash of a mouth there were only two holes where the nose should be and smooth skin above it. It had no eyes. Harper tried to scream but couldn't. She held Wisdom before her and rang it loudly, causing the creature to hold its hands to its ears and bellow with rage.

"Now, Harper!" Grandma Lee shouted.

They both launched into the binding prayer, invoking the wills of the Ancient One and the Worthy One.

"Through the power of the Ancient One, I bind you. You will do no harm. Through the power of the Worthy One, I bind you. You will do no harm. Through the power of the Ancient One, I bind you. You will do no harm. Through the power of the Worthy One, I bind you. You will do no harm."

Over and over they chanted, ringing the bells in unison.

"Harper! Harper! Help me!"

It was Rose's voice. Harper stopped midchant and jumped to her feet, clutching her binder bells.

"Rose, where are you?"

"Harper, no!" Her grandmother grabbed her hand. "It's a trick! It has broken our chant. We must start all over again!"

Furious with herself, Harper sat back down. But the creature had vanished. The room began to break apart, the house collapsing around them. The illusion felt so real, Harper coughed from the fumes of dust she breathed in. But she didn't stop chanting.

Suddenly, Rose appeared before her, her red hair flying all about her and her pretty face grimacing in terror.

"Harper! Stop! You're destroying me!"

Harper faltered, but her grandmother slapped her hard on the back of her head. *You're not real*, Harper thought to herself as she kept chanting. The house was engulfed in flames, and the smoke was so thick it became hard to breathe, and yet they still chanted. Until finally, the soul eater stood before Harper again, frozen in place. Its distended belly was lit up, and the skin moved as if there was something within it trying to get out.

"Why isn't it gone?" Harper asked.

"It's not a spirit, it's a demon," Grandma Lee said.

Harper flinched. "There's a difference?"

"Yes. A spirit was once human, with human emotions. But a demon never was. It is pure evil."

"But what is it really?" Harper asked, her voice rising.

"Not now, Harper!" Grandma Lee admonished. She was walking around the creature, studying it. "We've only bound it momentarily. Now we must release the spirits trapped within it, and that will kill it."

"How do we do that?" Harper tried not to panic as she stared in horror at the pulsating belly of the soul eater.

"We must focus all of our spiritual connections with the spirits ingested by the demon," Grandma Lee said. "We must reach out to them and help them escape."

"But how?"

"By leading them to the light," Grandma Lee said.

Harper gasped. "But Rose . . ."

Grandma gripped Harper's hand. "Would you

rather your friend spent eternity in the belly of that thing, having all of her energy used up until she is gone?"

Harper was crying, but she shook her head.

"Then help me free your friend!"

Grandma Lee pulled out two bells that Harper had never seen before. They were large and heavy.

"This is the Bringer, the Blessed One," Grandma Lee said as she held it in her right hand. With her left hand, she took hold of the larger bell. "This is the Unmaker, the Righteous One. This will be the last bell we ring to destroy the creature."

Harper nodded.

"Quickly—already the binding spell is coming apart!" Harper could see the soul eater beginning to twitch its long limbs.

Harper continued to ring her binding bells of Wisdom and Truth while Grandma Lee rang the Bringer and her strong alto voice called out.

"Come forth, dear ones! Come to the light and be free!" With every chant, they rang their bells in unison, the melodic toll breaking through the darkness of the room. A white light began to appear above their heads. The spirits within the soul eater started to pulse and surge, eager to reach the light.

"Come to the light and be free!"

They were chanting faster as the monster writhed in agony. The spirits within it were trying desperately to escape.

Suddenly, the face of the soul eater changed to that of Rose's.

"Harper! What are you doing? I thought I was your best friend! But now you're killing me!"

Tears streamed down the false Rose's face.

Harper couldn't help it. She wavered. And in that moment the creature broke free of the binding spell and lurched forward, reaching a clawed hand toward Harper. From behind her, Grandma Lee threw a bowl of holy water into the demon's face. It shrieked in pain.

"Once more, Harper, and don't stop, no matter what!"

With increasing urgency, they sang the song of release as they rang the shaman bells. The soul eater's belly suddenly ruptured as a stream of ghosts flew out of its body and began to float up toward the light.

"Now the Unmaker!"

With one hard shake, Grandma Lee rang the Unmaker, causing the soul eater to break apart, falling to pieces on the ground.

The air all around them was filled with happy

spirits, grateful to be free. They flew around and danced before soaring up into the light.

Thank you. Harper, thank you.

Familiar voices whispered their thanks. Harper recognized all the missing ghosts from the cemetery. For once, Mrs. Taylor didn't have her knitting with her, and Roderick was holding little Phoebe's hand. They waved at Harper, their smiles brighter than she'd ever seen them before. She waved back, happy to see them set free, but she was desperate to see only one person.

One bright light began to crystallize in front of her.

Harper let out a joyous shout at the sight of her friend before her. "Rose, you're okay! I was so worried about you."

There was the glimmer of tears on Rose's ghostly face.

"Harper, I'm so glad to see you again!"

The two friends embraced, and Harper felt warmth and softness, but her arms slipped through her friend's form.

Rose looked up at the beam of light and the amorphous forms of spirits steadily rising toward it.

"You know I can't stay," Rose said. "The pull of the light is too strong."

"But I just got you back!" Harper could no longer stop her tears. "This isn't fair! I can't lose you again!"

"I don't want to leave you, either," Rose cried.

Harper was sobbing. "Please don't go, Rose."

A ghostly hug surrounded her once more before Rose's form was pulled away.

"My one and only friend," Rose said. "I will always love you."

"No, Rose!" Harper begged. "Please don't go yet! Stay a little longer! I promise we'll get the light again, but not now! Please. Not yet."

Rose looked agonized. "It's too strong. I can't fight it. Good-bye, Harper! One day I'll see you again!"

Her radiant form flew up into the light to join the rest of the free spirits.

"No, no!" Harper sobbed. "You can't leave me."

And then the ghostly forms disappeared. Harper gazed at the light until it also faded away.

"I love you, Rose," Harper whispered.

Wiping away her tears, she turned to see her grandmother throwing holy water onto the remains of the soul eater. Steam rose into the air, and soon there was nothing but a dark stain on the wood floor.

Misery and exhaustion plagued Harper. It felt like her heart was breaking into a thousand pieces.

"I'll take care of cleaning this up," her grandmother said. "Why don't you go next door and send over those busybody ladies to come and help me."

Leaving the house, Harper was shocked to find the afternoon sun still shining brightly. It felt like she'd been inside the house for hours. She walked with a heavy heart. Her best friend was gone forever, just when she'd finally gotten her back.

MISSING ROSE
Friday, October 13

The days and nights without Rose passed without registering much with Harper. When she'd broken the news to Michael, he'd cried and sat on the bench in front of Rose's mirror in the foyer for an hour.

"I didn't get to say good-bye," he sobbed.

Harper stayed next to him the entire time, trying not to cry herself as she shared her memories of Rose. Her heart ached.

By the time Dayo came to see her, Harper was exhausted. As she explained what had happened, her words kept getting caught in her throat.

"I'm so sorry," Dayo said. "I know how much you're going to miss her."

Harper swallowed back a sob. "Grandma Lee said that I had to think about Rose and that she was in a much better place. And I know I'm being selfish, but I wish she could have stayed a little longer."

Dayo offered up sympathy and lots of her mother's cookies. Too sad to eat, Harper gave all the cookies to Michael.

Harper slid into a quiet solitude that her parents didn't know how to break. Grandma Lee had spoken to them about what had happened in a way that, as she put it, they could understand. And it seemed like Harper's parents were trying to accept what Grandma Lee explained to them. It had been hard enough to accept that the imaginary friend Harper had always played with was a ghost named Rose. Harper could tell there was also some relief for them, to know that Rose was gone, as if that would somehow make Harper normal. That was how she knew they didn't really understand.

Even Kelly, who was usually clueless and self-absorbed, seemed to be trying to be nicer to Harper, going out of her way to offer to drive her places. But Harper didn't want to go anywhere. She mostly stayed in her room, missing Rose, thinking of all the time they'd lost because of Harper's accident and her memory loss. Before Harper's family moved down to Washington, D.C., they'd lived in New York City, where Harper was possessed by a ghost who caused her to start a fire at her school. Because of the incident, Harper was sent to Briarly, a mental health institute for children. It was at Briarly that Harper was attacked by an angry, violent ghost. She was injured so badly she lost her memory and forgot all about Rose, something she couldn't even imagine now.

Harper thought back to the moment when she remembered Rose again.

"Harper, I've been so worried about you!" Rose rushed out *of the mirror and grabbed Harper in a ghostly embrace that felt like being squished between soft clouds. "I thought you would never remember me again!"*

Harper could still recall the overwhelming rush of love and affection she felt at the sight of her friend. *"Rose, I've missed you so much and I didn't even know it!"*

"And how do you think I felt? I could see you every day but never talk to you," Rose said. "It was like going back to the dark days."

The dark days were the days when Rose was trapped in the mirror with no one to speak to. Only now could Harper truly understand how hard it must have been for Rose. She'd just lost her best friend forever, and her heart hurt so much.

Her mother knocked and entered Harper's room, not waiting for a response. Harper gave her a dirty look. She didn't want to talk to anyone.

"Listen, I was trying to think of ways to make this trip more fun for you . . ."

Harper didn't respond. Her heart was heavy from the loss of her friend. That her mother was talking to her about a trip she didn't want to take at all seemed cruel.

Her mother cleared her throat and said, "Actually, I think I came up with a great idea— something I think even you will love. Want to know what it is?"

Harper shrugged. Nothing her mother said could make her feel better.

"Dayo's mom said it would be okay for Dayo to come on the trip with us."

At first Harper didn't think she'd heard right. "Dayo can come with us . . . ?" she repeated slowly.

Her mother smiled and nodded. Despite herself, Harper couldn't help but smile too. Having Dayo on the trip would make things so much better. Not because she could replace Rose—no one could ever do that. But because Dayo understood what Harper's parents couldn't.

Harper and Dayo stood in front of the foyer mirror staring sadly at their reflections. Dayo put a comforting arm around Harper's shoulders.

"It's hard to believe I won't ever see her again," Dayo said.

Harper let out a shaky breath and wiped her eyes. "I miss her so much."

"Me too," Dayo said.

"She used to tell me the best stories about all the strange things she'd seen," Harper remembered. "We'd play hide-and-seek for hours. Even though she could always find me, she would make it so much fun."

"I loved her singing," Dayo said. "She had the prettiest voice. And she could really rock a Beyoncé song."

Harper giggled. "But boy, was she bad at rapping."

Dayo laughed. "I loved that she'd still try."

After several long minutes of silence, Harper led Dayo away, and they shuffled over to the kitchen to raid the shelves. Dayo stared at the overflowing pantry in amazement.

"Every time I come over, you always have new stuff," she said in awe.

The pantry was filled not only with veggie chips and weird health food that her sister insisted on eating but also Asian snacks only found in Korean supermarkets.

Dayo pointed at something with Korean lettering that had a picture of a squid on it. "What's that?"

"Dried squid," Harper said. "But I don't think you'll like that. Let's have some Pepero instead."

She reached up to grab the big box of Korean chocolate-covered cookie sticks and let loose an avalanche of little packages that fell on both of their heads. Dayo was giggling madly when she grabbed one of the small packages. "Hey, I'll have some of this dried seaweed," she said. "What do you call it again—*kim*?"

"Yep, but I don't know if I have any rice," Harper said.

"I don't need rice," Dayo replied, ripping into the package and eating the thin black papery squares like potato chips.

Harper shook her head. "That's just wrong, eating *kim* without rice."

Dayo smiled. "Mmmm, salty!"

"Hey!" Harper exclaimed. "Look at this! I think I found my dad's secret stash of junk food."

She pulled down a box of Twinkies, Double Stuf

Oreos, and a bag of crunchy cheese puffs. They'd all been hidden deep behind the pile of dried seaweed packages.

"Cheese puffs!" Dayo crowed. "My mom never lets me eat those. She says they're too messy and too fake."

"That's why they taste so good," Harper replied.

"I'm so excited to go on this trip with you," Dayo said.

Harper smiled. "I didn't want to go at all, but now I'm actually looking forward to it!"

"Why? Don't you like the beach?" Dayo asked as she licked the creme out of her Oreo.

Harper shrugged. "I don't care about it one way or the other. I just can't stand my cousin Leo."

"That's the cousin who pranks you, right?"

"Yeah, and his last one was unforgivable. They came to visit in August right before school started," Harper said. "You were lucky to miss him."

"Oh, that was when I went to Georgia to visit my grandparents," Dayo said. "I remember you had Rose scare him to death."

Harper grinned. Leo had been pulling pranks on her every time they would meet during family reunions. It was the first time she'd ever retaliated.

"He deserved it. My uncle Justin makes the best

pastries, and his cream puffs are my favorite. He made me and Michael a big box of them, but Leo filled them with mayonnaise instead."

Dayo gasped in outrage. "That's despicable!"

"I almost threw up," Harper said. "I was so mad."

Harper remembered how excited they'd been to get the cream puffs. For once she'd felt complete goodwill toward Leo. The first bite was just awful. The taste was so disgusting that it had made Harper gag and Michael cry. And that was something Harper could not forgive. Even Michael, who was the sweetest kid, had approved of getting back at Leo with Rose's haunting.

"So, what did Rose do?" Dayo asked.

"We waited until midnight, and then Rose put on that horrible clown mask that my dad has in his closet."

Dayo shuddered. "Clowns are evil."

Harper nodded. "She floated right in Leo's face, wearing the clown mask, until he woke up. He was screaming like a baby."

The girls laughed.

"He definitely deserved it," Dayo said. "But won't that make him want to get you back even more?"

Harper shrugged. "Nothing he could do could ever compare to a real ghost haunting."

Dayo nodded but looked perplexed. "Still, I can't believe Rose agreed to do it. She was such a nice person."

"She would never have agreed to it normally," Harper said. "But she got so mad after the cream-puff incident."

Harper could see Rose's reaction in her memory. She had glowed bright with anger and had agreed immediately to Harper's plan.

"Rose was the kindest person in the entire world," Harper whispered. "Even though she agreed to do it, she felt really bad afterward. Leo was so scared."

But Harper didn't tell Dayo what Rose had said to her: "I never want to scare anyone like that again. I felt like I did something really wrong, and I don't like that feeling."

Harper had felt guilty ever since.

"Well, it will be interesting to meet your cousin," Dayo said.

Harper grimaced. She wasn't looking forward to it.

AT GRANDMA'S HOUSE
Thursday, October 26

The day before their Halloween trip to the Caribbean, Harper and Michael spent the night at their grandmother's house. Although Grandma Lee had invited Kelly also, Kelly had been too worried about packing to come over. But Harper was surprised when Kelly offered to drive them without their mom asking first.

"Stop making that face, Harper," Kelly said. "You're lucky to have me."

Michael giggled. "Harper, you look so funny."

Harper closed her gaping mouth and got in the car. "What's the catch?"

"I felt like it," Kelly said with a shrug. "Besides, this way I can see Grandma before we leave."

As they drove up to the small white house, Grandma was standing at the door waving.

"Grandma always knows when we are coming," Michael said with a happy grin.

Inside, Kelly gave Grandma a big hug but turned down dinner. "I've still got a lot of laundry to do before I can even pack," she said as she ran out the door.

Harper and Michael sat on the floor to give Monty lots of love. The little dog was ecstatic to see them and kept running back and forth between them. Grandma Lee quickly called them to dinner, where a platter full of Harper's favorite *kalbi*, grilled short ribs, sat center stage.

"Harper, your mama is worried about you," Grandma Lee said as they were eating dinner. "She says you only have Dayo as a friend and haven't made any others yet. And if Dayo is busy, you don't do anything but stay at home and mope."

Harper tried to swallow her food around the large lump that had formed in her throat. She put down her chopsticks, no longer hungry.

"But Grandma! Harper doesn't like to go out," Michael said. "She likes to be with me."

"Of course! Everybody loves you. But your sister needs more friends," Grandma said.

Harper looked away, resentment crawling up her throat. A feeling of betrayal churned within her. She'd just lost her best friend in the whole world. Wasn't she allowed to grieve? Couldn't she be left alone? She loved Dayo and was really glad to be friends with her, but she hadn't met anyone else at school that she had clicked with. Why did everyone think making friends was so easy? It wasn't. It was complicated and difficult, especially in middle school.

Grandma Lee was looking at her with sympathetic eyes. Suddenly she reached over and gave Harper a big hug. "I promised your mama I would say all that, but don't you even worry about it! You are a wonderful girl, and you will make many friends in your life. I'm not worried about you."

"Harper is the best," Michael said, his mouth full of rice and meat. "She's my favoritest person in the whole world, next to Mommy and Daddy and Grandma. And Kelly, when she's in a good mood. And Dayo, and my best friend Jacob, and my teacher Mrs. Burton, and my soccer coach—"

Before he could continue, Harper covered his mouth with her hand. "Little dude, you like everyone."

After dinner, Harper read Michael several chapters of his current favorite book, about a lonely robot, before tucking him into bed. Once he was asleep, she walked down the hall to the last room, the shrine room of the gods. Grandma Lee was a good Catholic who went to mass every Sunday. She once told Harper that she was Catholic before she ever became a shaman. Mrs. Devereux joked about how horrified Grandma's priest, Father Rios, would be if he ever saw the shrine room. However, Grandma Lee believed that communing with nature as a shaman was not incompatible with being a good Christian.

As a shaman, it was her job to lead the spirits that came to her back to the light. It wasn't always an easy task, especially when the spirits were lost or unwilling. Harper knew people sought her grandmother only when they were in desperate need. She never charged money for her services, but money always came to her. Her pantry overflowed with food, and her closets were filled with presents from grateful clients. They would also leave her envelopes full of cash.

The shrine door was open, and Harper could see her grandmother kneeling before the altar, jade prayer beads clasped tightly in her hands as she chanted. Bowls of fruit and candy adorned the altar table. She remembered how her grandmother had laughed when she'd found out that Michael had eaten all the Snickers miniatures one night. "The child gods will be so upset that all they are getting are peppermints tonight," she'd said.

The room was beautifully decorated, with a large painted fan displayed on a stand. There were drums and cymbals, and several vases of flowers that looked so real but were completely fake. On the wall behind the altar hung colorful paintings of the mountain deity San-shin, the ocean deity Bada-shin, and Princess Bari, the first female shaman. The walls next to the altar displayed various Korean costumes. A child's *hanbok* as well as one that could be worn by royalty hung on either side of the altar, while the old armor of an ancient general was showcased on the opposite wall. On the floor before the altar stood a large *janggu*, a double-headed hourglass drum. Michael was fascinated by the drum, always wanting to bang on it.

"Grandma, why is it that Mom and Dad don't want to believe in ghosts?"

Harper sat next to her grandmother in the shrine room, helping her take down and polish the old general's leather armor.

"You see, some people have a very strong spiritual connection, like you and your brother. Others, like your sister and your father, have a very slight connection, which makes them aware of things but skeptical," her grandmother said. "And then there are those whose minds are so completely shut off from the spiritual world that they are nonbelievers."

"Like Mom," Harper said.

"Like your mother," her grandmother agreed. "But she is trying. Michael's possession by that ghost really shook your mother up. She's more like your dad now. She recognizes something happened. But she's not quite ready to name it what it really is."

When they had first moved into their new house, there had been a little boy ghost who had possessed Michael, changing him into a monster. It had been the most frightening experience of Harper's life, because she was so afraid for her brother.

"Sometimes I think Mom wishes I was more like Kelly," Harper said.

Grandma Lee put down her polishing rag and stroked her hand through Harper's hair.

"My dear girl, your mother loves you deeply," she said. "She is frustrated because she does not understand, and that frightens her. This is just the way things have always been. People fear what they don't comprehend."

"You mean she's scared of me?"

"Not of you, but of what her mind cannot accept. People will shut themselves off so completely to the world of possibilities that everything to them becomes only black or white. They try to explain everything away with some kind of rational explanation. But when they can't, it frightens them—because it shakes their core belief system that life is what you see, with no mysteries."

The explanation didn't really make sense to Harper. If anything, it depressed her. How could her mother ever come to understand her if she couldn't see the world as it truly was?

"Well, I know they are trying," Harper said. "But it feels awkward. Like they're pretending to believe something just to make me feel better, but it only makes me feel weird."

"Give them time, Harper," Grandma Lee said. "It has only been a few months since they found out that a ghost possessed their youngest child and almost killed him. They are still processing all of this."

Harper shrugged. "Okay, but I hate that Kelly acts like nothing weird ever happened this past summer."

Grandma Lee gave a little chuckle. "I'm not so sure that Kelly is as oblivious as she pretends to be. Something tells me she is more aware than we know."

Harper snorted in disbelief, earning her a chastising glance from her grandmother.

"Sometimes it's easier to pretend everything is all right rather than face your fears and your mistakes," she said. "Especially if you've spent your entire life making fun of your younger sister for believing in something that you are now not so sure about."

Harper shrugged. She wasn't really interested in psychoanalyzing her sister. Kelly was just Kelly.

They were quiet for several minutes, when Harper asked her grandmother about something that had been troubling her.

"That soul-eater demon," she said, suppressing a shudder. "You said a demon was not the same as a spirit, because a spirit was once a human and a demon was not."

Grandma Lee nodded.

"Then what is a demon? What is that soul-eater thing?"

Grandma Lee gazed at the altar. "It is an evil creature as old as time itself," she said. "I only know a little bit about them. They were once treated as gods and given numerous human sacrifices until a great shaman banished them into the spirit realm. Nowadays, a soul eater might slip into our world from time to time. But no one knows where they come from or how they get here."

The image of the pale no-eyed soul eater appeared in Harper's mind, raising goose bumps all over her arms. She'd seen a lot of scary ghosts in her short life, but the soul eater was by far the scariest thing she'd ever seen. She hoped she'd never see another ever again.

They finished polishing the armor when her grandmother froze, her head cocked to the side as if listening to something.

"What is it, Grandma? Who's talking to you?"

Her grandmother didn't answer. Her eyes had turned inward, and she looked as if she were in another world. Harper sat quietly, waiting until her grandmother returned to herself.

Several long moments later, her grandmother moved again. Immediately, her hands began to rub her prayer beads between them.

"Who was that?" Harper asked.

"Mrs. Devereux," her grandmother whispered.

"Is she coming now?" Harper asked, as she looked around the room. She liked Mrs. Devereux but found her quite intimidating. She was a very old and extremely powerful spirit originally from New Orleans. She was once a witch and a psychic, who could read a person's thoughts and curse them in the same moment.

"I'd asked her to go and check Razu Island out, to find out if it is safe for my grandchildren. But she tells me that she can't access it, that she's scared to do so without a medium."

"What does that mean?"

"A medium is anyone with the ability to channel spiritual energy directly, like you and me," her grandmother said. "In this case, she doesn't want to venture into an area without that protected channel, because she fears she might not come back."

Harper's mind immediately turned to Rose and the soul eater. "She's afraid of something that is down there."

"Furthermore, she can't call any spirits there to talk to. She calls it a spiritual wasteland," Grandma said. "I wish there was a way to cancel this trip."

Harper shook her head hard. "No way—Mom would freak out big time if you even try to mention it to her. She's been looking forward to this trip for months! It's Uncle Justin and Aunt Caroline's big celebration weekend for their jobs."

Grandma sighed. "I don't know what to do. I want to go with you, but I need to go to New York for your aunt Youjin's baby. This will be a difficult birth, and she is going to need my help." Regret and fear tinged her voice.

Harper was worried. If her grandmother was troubled, then she was, too. It meant that something was not right there spiritually.

"When you arrive, you must call in Madame Devereux so she can investigate the island safely," her grandmother said.

Harper nodded. Her grandmother had taught her the safe and correct way to call a spiritual adviser, using her shaman bowls.

Mrs. Devereux was the coolest and most dangerous spirit Harper knew. If there was something that even she was wary of, then Harper was downright scared to death.

MURDER IN PARADISE

Friday, October 27

Harper had to admit that it was refreshing to breathe in the salty sea air after a three-hour delay and a two-and-a-half-hour flight to Miami International Airport. The ferry they were on was filled with happy, excited families eager to start their vacations. Harper and Dayo were holding Michael up between them as he oohed and aahed over swimming dolphins and the waves that splashed up high. Her parents were off to the side, talking with Uncle Justin, who had met them at the airport.

The sound of her brother's laughter caught her

attention. He was waving his hands over the railing, letting the sea spray hit them.

"Harper, look at the dolphins!" He lurched forward, almost falling out of their arms and into the water.

Dayo and Harper gasped in horror. They pulled him back and placed him safely on the deck.

"That's it for you, little buddy! We can't have you falling in before we even get to the island," Harper said.

"Why? I can swim!" he said indignantly.

"Yes, but I don't want to," Harper retorted. "Neither does Dayo. And we all know there's no way Kelly's jumping in after you."

They all glanced over to where Kelly was animatedly flirting with a cute boy.

"Kelly talks too much." Michael grinned. "I know, let's push her over by accident!"

"You can't do that," Harper said. "She'd pull us all in with her."

"Then I'd get to swim!" Michael grinned.

Harper laughed and leaned over to pick him up and give him a big squeeze as he pointed in glee at the dolphin pod swimming alongside the boat. She noticed Dayo gazing wistfully at them.

"What's the matter?" she asked over Michael's head.

Dayo shrugged. "Sometimes I wish I had a little brother or sister, too."

Michael reached over to Dayo and climbed into her arms. "It's okay, Dayo, I can be your little brother also," he said. "You can share me."

"Thank you, little brother," Dayo said.

"Look!" Michael shouted. "It's the island!"

"You're supposed to say 'Land ho!'" Harper teased.

"Land ho!" Michael shouted, loud enough to cause the people around them to turn and smile.

In the distance, Harper could see the marina filled with bright sails and the outline of the island behind it. A cold wind whipped through her hair, sending a shiver down her spine. Despite the colorful tropical paradise ahead, Harper could feel goose bumps appearing all over her arms.

With Rose's absence, Harper had been depressed. Worse, she couldn't shake the uneasy sense she'd gotten ever since talking to her grandmother. Something about this trip had spooked Grandma Lee.

Harper had done a little bit of internet research into Razu and wasn't surprised to find that the island had a violent past. It had been a deserted island until

Montgomery Bennington, the hotel mogul, had discovered it in 1912 as a young man. But it took eight years to open the first Grande Bennington Hotel Resort and Beach Club. There was some shady business involved during the construction of the resort, and allegations of murder trailed Bennington. But he had become too rich and powerful for anyone to confront him. When he died in his eighties in 1970, the hotel chain passed on to his eldest son, Samuel Bennington, who was fifty at the time but had no children of his own. At his death, twenty years later, the hotel chain passed to the only remaining Bennington heir, Sam's much younger half sister's son, Todd Bennington, who was only twenty at the time. It was during Todd's ownership that the real tragedy occurred. Sixteen people were murdered in a horrible manner, including a very young child. The murders tainted the hotel's reputation, and people stopped coming. The hotel fell into disrepair, and even other Bennington hotels began to suffer globally. Strange things would happen. One would burn down, and another would have some scandal. It was as if the Bennington name had been cursed and the family plagued with both personal and business disasters. And then suddenly Todd Bennington deserted his pregnant wife and vanished. Rumor had it that he stole his wife's jewelry and the last of the family cash.

But fourteen years later, the Bennington name was gold again and the company a financial powerhouse. Todd's wife, Clarissa Bennington, had taken over control of the company and brought it back from financial ruin. She even reinvested in the Grande Hotel, ordering a major remodeling that took several years to complete. This grand opening was supposed to be the most lavish celebration, meant to make people forget all about the grisly murders that happened years ago. But for Harper, the murders weighed heavily on her mind.

The sun was beginning its descent as they joined the throng of tourists leaving the boat. Dayo and Harper held Michael's hands tightly as Uncle Justin herded them down the ramp and out onto the pier. They followed him to a hotel shuttle bus. The driver was already loading their suitcases into the back.

"Okay guys, we'll go straight to the hotel so you can hit the beach or pool while it's still light," Uncle Justin said. "Leo will be happy to see you all."

Harper snorted and Michael grinned at her. She seriously doubted that.

"You think he's going to pull a prank on us?" Dayo whispered.

"Not if he knows what's good for him," Harper whispered back.

Her mother poked her lightly in the side. "Now, Harper, you be nice," she said with a warning gaze.

Harper suppressed a sigh. It wasn't like she could do anything really scary to Leo anymore. Not without Rose.

A pain shot through her at the thought of her oldest friend. Almost every day Harper wanted to share something with Rose, only to be reminded that she was gone. It made her heart hurt.

She sat in the very back of the bus with Dayo and Michael, behind the rest of her family.

"So, did you hear about the murders that happened here?" Kelly asked.

Dayo's eyes grew wide. "No—what happened?"

"They say it was a satanic cult, because the thirteen bodies were found in a circle around the trees, and their insides had been pulled out of their bodies."

"I thought there were sixteen victims," Harper interjected.

"Yeah, that's right, but three were outside of the circle, as if they just happened upon the murderer and then they were killed, too."

"Kelly, enough with the rumors," their father said in a warning voice.

"Sorry," Kelly said. "Hey, Uncle Justin, will we get to see the place they disappeared from?"

Harper noticed how tight Uncle Justin's jaw got. Before he could respond, the shuttle driver spoke up.

"You talking about Gorgon Grove, missy? That's one scary place," he said. "We'll be driving past it. You can see the back part of the grove right from the road."

"Cool!" Kelly said. "I hear that it's the most haunted place in the world. They say you can still hear the cries for help from the trees."

"Okay, that's enough," their mother said. "It's just some silly superstitions. Don't go scaring your brother like that."

"Don't worry about him. Nothing scares him, right, Mikey?" Kelly asked.

"I ain't scared of nothin'! But don't call me Mikey!"

Harper hid her smirk. Kelly was always trying to give them cute pet names that they both resented— although Kelly's nickname for Harper was not so cute. The last time Kelly had called her Harpy, she'd put baby powder in Kelly's hair dryer.

Kelly was looking at her map of the island. She pointed at a section marked *Gorgon Grove*. "Here it is," she said. "Looks like it's going to be on our left side."

Harper repressed a shudder, because she knew from experience that most of the time the spirits of victims would haunt their last resting places. If something bad had happened, then the spiritual energy would be strong here, especially for those who were sensitive to it.

Dayo shivered and whispered into Harper's ear, "Are there going to be ghosts there?"

"Probably," Harper said. She looked down at Michael. He was still so little. She worried about what he might see.

"Hey, Michael, you want to play your Nintendo again?" Harper asked. Michael nodded excitedly, turning on his *Super Mario Kart* race game.

Harper sat back with a sigh of relief. Hopefully, her brother would be too absorbed in the game to notice anything. The shuttle bus began to drive along a narrow coastal road before cutting up into the heart of the island. Here, the jungle canopy was heavy, shading them from the sun. But the air was thick and muggy. There was a sense of isolation within the trees. A feeling that they'd entered into another world and another time.

"Creepy," Kelly said.

Harper nodded. She noted a negative aura, which was getting stronger.

Michael's hand suddenly grasped hers tightly. She looked down and saw his frightened expression.

"It's okay, just play your game. Close your mind up. Remember what I taught you?" she whispered. He nodded solemnly, his eyes never wavering from her face. "Focus on the game and close off all the other senses until it's safe, okay?"

He turned back to the game in earnest, his little fingers pressing the keys to make the race car go.

Harper looked up and noted Dayo's wide eyes. "Do you sense something, too?" she asked her.

"I'm not sure," Dayo said. "But something feels really creepy."

Harper noticed that the oppressive feeling was stronger than ever. It almost felt like it was right on top of her. And then she saw it. Gorgon Grove. Twisted, deranged, and unnatural. It was the trees that gave off the sense of menace and danger, nearly pulsating with it. There was no doubting that this was the place, but there were no ghosts haunting it. No sign of spiritual residue. Harper was relieved and yet confused. This made no sense. How could a site with such a negative aura be ghost free? She wished her grandmother were with her—she would know what to do.

Glancing down at her brother, she noticed that

he was focusing hard on the game and was paying no attention to their whereabouts. But both Dayo and Kelly were staring in horrified fascination at the trees. Kelly pulled out her camera and began taking pictures.

"Wow, they are so freaky!" Kelly said, still clicking her camera as they drove away. "I hope we don't ever see them again."

"Which is why you took a hundred pictures of them," Harper said.

"That's different! I want to show everyone the pictures of where the murders occurred, but I don't want to experience it again. It felt oppressive," Kelly said. She shuddered, making Harper realize that maybe her older sister had some spiritual powers that she was not even aware of.

"Kelly, do you ever see ghosts?" Harper asked.

Her sister gazed at her in disbelief. "What? Are you for real?" she asked. "Seriously, Harper. It's one thing for Michael to talk about ghosts, but you're nearly thirteen. Stop being a baby."

"Kelly, what about this past summer? What about Michael? What do you think happened to him?"

"I really don't want to talk about it," Kelly said with an angry glare.

And just like that, her feeling of kinship with Kelly faded. Harper sighed. It was going to be a long vacation.

Dayo gave Harper a sympathetic smile and whispered, "I have to admit, I'm real glad I wasn't touching you, Harper. I wouldn't have wanted to see any ghosts in there." She shuddered. "I was so scared just looking at the trees."

Dayo could only see ghosts if she was touching Harper. Grandma Lee said Harper's abilities were so great she could channel the spirit realm for energy to move things around without ever touching them. But Harper still hadn't been able to do it. Grandma Lee promised that it would come with time and practice. Harper couldn't wait.

Harper frowned. "That's the funny thing. There were no ghosts there."

"Where'd they go?"

Staring out the window, Harper couldn't help but think about what Grandma Lee had said. "I don't know," Harper responded.

They'd arrived at the resort, driving past a gigantic sign proclaiming that it was a Bennington hotel. The shuttle bus entered through a palm tree–lined driveway that circled the front of a Spanish-style mansion with a red-tile roof and a large archway supported by Grecian columns. They alighted on a brick walkway framed by a dazzling display of hibiscus, hanging orchids, pink powder puffs, and cloud-like purplish-pink ornamental grass that grew in large clumps. Michael jumped out of the bus and began chasing the small yellow geckos that covered the ground.

It was picture-postcard beautiful, and yet the closer Harper got to the entranceway, the colder she felt. She noticed that all the little geckos her brother was chasing fled away from the building, even circling around to avoid coming too close. A sudden chill overcame her. The geckos had the right idea. There was a negative aura about the building that spoke of tragedy and fear. She had to will her feet to move her forward. At the doorway, Michael clutched Harper's hand tightly.

"I don't think I like this place," he whispered. "I'm afraid."

Harper nodded and grasped his hand, wishing she'd been able to pull out her backpack that held her shaman bells. On her other side, Dayo had a vise grip on Harper's arm.

"What is it?" Dayo asked. "Are there ghosts here?"

Harper closed her eyes, breathed deeply, and channeled her sixth sense. It sprang to life and prodded at her. She opened her eyes again and saw the lobby anew, ready to see beyond the physical plane. Scanning the room, she was surprised to find nothing out of the ordinary. Bellboys in bright flower-print shirts pushed carts filled with bags as uniformed staff directed their guests. On the other side of the room were sofas and oversized armchairs, all filled with people sitting and drinking.

"Do you see anything special?" Harper asked her little brother. He shook his head. Strange, she thought. There were no ghosts in the vicinity, and yet she could feel the echoes of their emotions—fear, anguish, anger, rage. It was troubling, to say the least. Looking down at her brother, she noticed that his face was pale and his eyes were large.

"Are you okay, Michael?" she asked.

He nodded. "This place is bad."

"But do you feel okay?"

"My head hurts a little, and I'm hungry," he said.

"We'll get you some food soon enough, kiddo!" Uncle Justin said as he walked over to them. He handed their father a pair of room key cards and ruffled Michael's hair. "I sent your bags on to our house, but let me show you around the resort first."

"Thanks, Justin—this is just the vacation we needed," Harper's mother said. She looked tired. Harper felt a pang of sympathy. She made a promise to herself to try not to upset her mom on the trip.

Justin smiled. "I'm glad you guys are here. It means a lot to us." He then turned to Harper, Kelly, and Michael, pointing outside to where the pools were located. "Hey, there's Leo. Why don't you kids go talk to him while I show your folks the casino?"

"Harper," her mother called out. "Be nice."

Harper rolled her eyes as she and the others walked out of the darkened glass doors of the lobby and into the large pool area. There were multiple pools, the biggest of which even had a large slide that kids were hurtling down with huge splashes. Michael was jumping up and down in excitement as they walked across to where their cousin was sitting.

At their approach, Leo stood to greet them. Harper swallowed back a gasp. It had been only a few months since she'd seen her cousin, and he'd changed drastically. He'd always been thin, but he'd lost so much weight that his blue eyes had sunk deep into their sockets and his pale skin was sallow. He was glaring at Harper with eyes filled with anger, fear, and a frantic sort of desperation.

"What happened to you?" Harper asked.

"You did this to me!" he said. "And you need to make it stop!"

LEO'S PROBLEM

Friday, October 27–Same day

Kelly rolled her eyes. "So dramatic, as always," she said. "Come on, Michael, let's go take a closer look at that slide."

"Oh boy!"

Harper stood awkwardly in front of Leo, unsure of what to do until Dayo gave her a nudge.

"Oh, yeah, so this is my best friend, Dayo Clayton. Dayo, this is my cousin Leo," Harper said. "And I have no idea what he's talking about."

"You know exactly what you did," Leo said through gritted teeth. "You cursed me, and now I'm haunted."

"Haunted?" Dayo asked. "What do you mean by that?"

"The last time I saw her, she cursed me and said something bad would happen. And then a ghost attacked me."

"No she didn't," Harper muttered.

"And ever since the summer, I see ghosts wherever I go. I can't make it stop."

Harper raised an eyebrow in surprise. "You mean you can see ghosts on your own now?"

"What do you mean, 'on my own'?"

"You never really saw a ghost at my house," Harper said. "It was just a floating clown mask."

"I'm telling you, I see ghosts! And it's your fault!"

He grabbed Harper by the arms. "You've gotta help me!"

The look of fear on Leo's face was so strong that Harper felt a sharp pang of guilt.

"I don't know how, Leo," she said. "I don't know if what you're seeing is even a real ghost."

"Of course it is! And it comes every night. I haven't been able to sleep since we got here!"

Harper let out a pained sign. "So, describe the ghost to me."

Leo ran a hand through his hair, making him

look demented. "There's this creepy little girl that shows up every night," he said with a shudder. "I feel like she keeps trying to talk to me, but I won't let her."

"Well, does she talk to you or not?" Harper asked.

Dayo nudged him again. "She means how is she trying to talk to you?"

"I don't know," Leo said, throwing up his hands. "She shows up at my bed every night! I just shut my eyes and cover my ears and talk loudly until she leaves."

Harper rolled her eyes. "So, you didn't even try to see what she wants to say to you?"

"Why would I want to talk to a ghost?"

"To find out why she keeps coming!"

Leo poked Harper hard in her shoulder. "This is all your fault."

Harper shoved his hand away and was ready to yell at him when Dayo stepped in between the two cousins.

"You keep saying that," she said. "But how can it be Harper's fault that you see ghosts?"

"Because I never saw them before that ghost haunted me at her house," he said, pointing at Harper.

"But how is that her fault?"

"She was laughing—I saw it!" he shouted. "And I saw the ghost wink at her before vanishing."

"Wait a minute, you saw Rose?" Harper asked incredulously.

"Who's Rose?"

"You saw her take off the mask?" Harper asked.

"At the very end, when you came to my room. I saw you laughing, and the ghost with the red hair winked before disappearing."

Dayo turned to Harper in surprise. "But I've been around lots of ghosts, and I still can't see them myself," she said. "I wonder why he can see them all of a sudden."

Harper shrugged, but felt a sinking sense of guilt as she realized her prank had caused real-life consequences for Leo.

"I'm sure we can figure out how to help you," Dayo said. She nudged Harper, who grudgingly agreed.

"I don't know how you got the ability in the first place. I could ask my grandma Lee, but without seeing you in person, I'm not sure what she could do."

"What about Mrs. Devereux?" Dayo asked.

Harper made a face. "You know I hate bothering her—"

"You'd better do it, or I'm going to make your life miserable," Leo cut in.

Harper glared. "You already do, maggot breath."

She would have kept going, but Dayo gave her a look.

"For Rose's sake, I'll help him," she muttered to Dayo.

They ate lunch at the hotel, and then Uncle Justin and Leo took them to their house. They rode in golf carts driven by hotel staff, and traveled down a long sandy road. The adults all rode in the first cart while the five kids all piled in the second cart. Kelly squeezed in between Dayo and Michael, leaving an unhappy Harper to sit with Leo.

"I guess Aunt Caroline is pretty important at the resort," Harper said to Leo.

"She is the vice president and general manager of the entire resort," Leo said proudly. "This house actually used to be where the Bennington family lived. But when Mr. Bennington deserted them, Mrs. Bennington took Olivia and moved to the other side of the resort. So, they gave it to us when we came here."

Just then the house came into view, and Harper

let out a loud whistle. "That's a mansion, Leo."

"Much nicer than your old decrepit house," Leo smirked.

Harper counted to ten silently to avoid pushing him off the cart.

Inside, Aunt Caroline finally appeared and gave them all excited hugs. Harper was so glad to see her. Her aunt Caroline was a tall, attractive woman, with thick brown hair she kept in a short bob.

"For dinner, we are going back to the hotel. There's a big banquet held for special guests on the private beach," Aunt Caroline said. "Don't worry, Kelly, there's even a separate event for young adults. You'll have a blast!"

Aunt Caroline then took them all up to their rooms. "This place is so big that you all can have your own rooms, but Harper, I thought you'd want to share with Dayo."

Harper and Dayo nodded enthusiastically as Aunt Caroline opened the door to a large room with two full-size beds in it.

"And your parents are just down the hall from you."

Michael immediately complained. "I don't wanna sleep by myself," he said. "Can I sleep with them, too?"

"You'll be right next to them," Aunt Caroline said. She opened the connecting door to a small room with a twin-size bed.

"Hey, we can leave the connecting door open!" Harper suggested. "Then it will be like one big sleepover."

Michael beamed happily. "That's even better!"

Harper and Dayo immediately went to unpack their bags, while Michael jumped onto a bed and stretched out. Leo stood hovering at the door.

"What?" Harper asked. He annoyed her just by breathing near her.

"My room is down at the other end of the hall."

"Like I care," Harper muttered.

"You promised to help me," Leo whined.

"Dude, we just got here. Please chill!"

Michael jumped off the bed and ran over to him. "I wanna see your room."

Harper rolled her eyes after the boys left. "Isn't he the worst?"

Dayo chuckled. "I definitely see why you're not friends, but I feel sorry for him. Don't you? We need to help him."

Harper pouted. She didn't want to do anything for him.

"It's what Rose would want you to do."

Harper heaved a big sigh. Dayo was right. Rose had felt so bad about how badly she'd scared him. She would feel terrible if she knew that their prank had left Leo so traumatized.

"Fine," Harper replied. "But you have to help me."

Dayo grinned.

A SURPRISE NEW FRIEND
Friday, October 27–Evening

They arrived to find the party was already going strong. Long picnic tables were filled with food and drinks. Hotel employees served the buffet, and there was even a large pavilion area with a dance floor. Kelly disappeared with a group of other teens wearing matching bikini tops and bright patterned skirts.

Harper and Dayo wandered over to the food table, which was covered with a vast array of island specialties. Grabbing two plates each, they loaded one up with pasta and meats, and the other with fresh seafood.

"Try the stone crabs—they're an island specialty," a voice said. "That is, if there's any room left on your plate."

Harper looked over to find a pretty girl with copper-red hair and bright blue eyes smiling at her. She reminded her of Rose so much that a pang of loneliness shot through her.

Dayo grinned back at the girl. "Our motto is that there is always room on our plate for good food, isn't that right, Harper?"

Harper nodded enthusiastically.

The redheaded girl raised her hand for a high five and then flushed, her pale freckled skin turning as red as her hair. "Okay, that was silly," she said. "Your hands are full."

Harper stuck out her elbow. They all knocked elbows before bursting into a fit of giggles.

"I'm Olivia Bennington," the redheaded girl said.

Harper's eyebrow raised. "As in the hotel?"

She nodded. "You're not going to hold that against me, are you?"

"Only if the food is bad," Harper said.

Dayo laughed. "And you have to eat as much as we do."

Olivia grinned at them. "I'll put you to shame."

"You're on!"

Olivia pushed back imaginary sleeves, grabbed two plates, and began to serve herself a mountain of food. Harper and Dayo shared a look of admiration before piling on even more for themselves. When there was no more space on any of their plates, Olivia led them to a quiet side table away from the festivities. As they sat, waiters served them drinks and separated them from the party, behind a large folding wall.

"Mmmm, this is so good!"

"Oh good, then you have to like me," Olivia replied.

"I wish I had grabbed more of these shrimpy things," Dayo said wistfully as she ate the last one.

Olivia called over a waiter and asked for more shrimp.

"Nice to be a Bennington," Dayo remarked.

"I'm not special. I'm just like you guys," Olivia replied.

Harper laughed. "Yeah, just like us, but with power!"

"So, are you here for the holiday?" Dayo asked.

"No, I live here," she replied.

"All year round?"

Olivia sighed. "Yeah, all my life. I've never been off the island, not even for a vacation. I've always wanted to go to New York City and see a real Broadway musical."

"How old are you?" Harper asked. "Your family owns hotels all over the world—how could you not have left?"

Olivia shrugged, resigned. "I don't know, my mom's been a bit paranoid. I don't think she trusts the world. I've never really gotten a good reason out of her. And I'm thirteen."

"Me too!" Dayo beamed. "And at least this place is really nice."

"Now it is," Olivia sighed. "You should have seen it before this summer. The hotel has been under renovation for ages. I live in a private house on the beach. I've been homeschooled all my life. The only friends I have are the ones that come on holiday. The village kids won't have anything to do with me because I'm a Bennington. And I have constant babysitters." She pointed out a few hotel employees who seemed to be standing around watching the scene. "It is the worst sort of prison you can imagine."

Harper and Dayo looked at each other, appalled. It didn't sound good at all.

"What about your dad?" Dayo asked. "Can't he take you off the island?"

Their new friend looked really sad. "My dad abandoned us before I was born."

"Oh, I'm so sorry," Dayo said. She reached over the table to pat Olivia on the hand.

Olivia smiled. "But I'm so glad I met you two. And for dessert there's a huge chocolate fountain that you can dip anything you want in."

"A chocolate fountain?" Harper began shoveling the rest of her food into her mouth as fast as she could. The girls laughed as they raced to finish their meals and then rushed over to the elaborate dessert table.

"It's beautiful," Harper sniffed, wiping away fake tears as she took in the enormous fountain of flowing chocolate surrounded by fruit, pieces of cake, cookies, and all sorts of other edible treats. "I have to show Michael."

Her parents were eating dinner with him in the dining room. Harper, Dayo, and Olivia wove their way inside, to find Michael sitting at the table with Leo and the adults. Michael looked terribly bored. His face lit up when he spotted Harper.

"Where were you?"

"There's a buffet area with a chocolate fountain!" Harper said. "We came back to get you!"

Michael hopped down and grabbed Harper's hand.

Before they could leave, Harper's aunt and uncle noticed who was with them.

"Oh Olivia, it is so nice to see you," Aunt Caroline said. "I see you've met my niece and her friend."

"Yes, thank you," Olivia answered with a polite smile. "I've been having a marvelous time with Harper and Dayo. We are going to gorge ourselves on the desserts, which look amazing, as always, Mr. Richmond."

Uncle Justin looked pleased. "Thank you, Olivia. All of you must tell me what your favorite dessert is."

"Will do," Harper chimed in. Then, before she could drag everyone away, she heard her mother say, "Leo, why don't you go with them?"

Leo shot Harper a dirty look, but reluctantly got up to join them. Harper looked at Dayo and rolled her eyes.

Michael chatted brightly with Olivia, telling her how much he loved chocolate, and all the things he hoped he would find to dip into it. Olivia listened politely and responded with seriousness. Harper and Dayo shared an approving look—they both liked

Olivia a lot. It was just too bad Leo had to come, too.

After filling up on chocolate-dipped treats of strawberries, pineapple, cookies, cakes, and other amazing delicacies, they were all given long sticks with marshmallows and sent out to roast them over bonfires manned by waitstaff.

"This is great!" Michael said. "I wish I could eat like this every day. You're so lucky, Olivia."

"Oh, this is special-occasion stuff," Olivia said. "I don't get to eat like this every day. That wouldn't be very healthy."

"Yeah, but it sure would taste good," Michael said.

"But you wouldn't be happy, because you'd get a stomachache every day," Leo retorted.

Michael glared at him. "You're just a grump." He stuck his tongue out at him as he made a loud raspberry sound.

The girls laughed. "Seriously, Leo, you need to lighten up," Harper said.

"Easy for you to say," Leo snapped. "You're not the one being haunted."

"Haunted?" Olivia said sharply. "What do you mean?"

Harper and Dayo traded looks. Harper didn't want Leo to scare Olivia off, but they couldn't stop him from launching into his story. He ended with telling them about the little ghost girl who was haunting him, appearing each night in his bedroom.

"Why don't you just talk to her?" Michael asked.

"Why would I want to talk to her?"

"To find out what she wants," Michael said. "Most ghosts just want to talk. They're lonely."

"Most ghosts?"

"Well, except for the ones that want to hurt you or take over your body," Michael continued.

Leo's face fell. He looked so appalled and shocked that Harper had to laugh. But then she noticed that Olivia looked upset also.

"Hey, guys, enough ghost talk," Harper said. "Look out on the beach! They've got light-up beach balls!"

"Can we go play, too?" Michael asked, jumping up and down.

Olivia smiled. "I'll get some," she said. Within a few moments, they each had a light-up beach ball and were seeing how long they could keep them in the air. They were all having a great time, even Leo, when a hotel staff member approached them.

"I'm sorry, Miss Bennington, but the sun is setting, and you know your mother wants you home by sunset."

"But it's only seven!" Harper replied. "Do you have to go so soon?"

Olivia looked rebellious at first and then resigned. "I have to go," she said. "My mom is very strict about my being home at sunset. It's like she's afraid of the dark or something." Olivia gave a weak smile. "But would you like to meet me for breakfast? I can take you snorkeling at a private beach!"

"That would be awesome!" Dayo said as Harper nodded.

"Brilliant!" Olivia said. "I'll send a hotel van to get you at eight a.m."

"Um, well, huh," Harper started to fuss, which made Olivia's smile fade a little.

"It's okay if you don't want to . . ."

Dayo busted out laughing. "It's not that at all. Harper can't get up that early. She is *not* a morning person."

Dayo gave Harper a nudge as Harper smiled sheepishly.

"I could be ready by nine! Is that okay?"

Olivia beamed. "Yes, that would be excellent! I'll see you in the morning!"

"Hey, what about me and Leo?" Michael pouted.

"Oh, you both can definitely come," Olivia said. "There's plenty of fun stuff to do, and there's even an instructor who can teach you how to snorkel!"

With a happy wave, Olivia quickly left with the waiting hotel staff.

As the kids walked back inside to join the grown-ups, Dayo whispered in Harper's ear. "Weird how her mom insists she's home at sunset, right?"

"Maybe she's a werewolf," Harper whispered.

"Or maybe rich people are just weird," Dayo said.

The girls laughed, as Leo glared at them.

"Okay, Leo, what do you want?"

"I want you to come and get rid of that ghost girl for me," he said.

Dayo and Harper exchanged glances and then nodded. "Okay, we'll do it."

"Tonight?" he asked hopefully.

"Tonight."

Michael clapped his hands. "Can I help, too?"

"Of course," Harper said. "You know a lot more about ghosts than Leo does."

Her dig didn't seem to bother Leo, who finally looked happy for the first time since they'd seen him. "She always appears at three a.m."

Harper groaned loudly, but Dayo gave her a look.

"Fine, but you have to come and wake us, okay?"

THE LITTLE GHOST
Saturday, October 28–Early morning

That night it wasn't Leo who woke them. It was Michael.

Harper opened her eyes as she felt small hands shaking her and giggling.

"Wake up, Harper!" Michael said.

She scowled at him and looked over to the clock. It was three in the morning.

"Where's Leo?" she asked.

"He's probably still asleep," Dayo replied as she came over to sit next to Harper.

"I thought he was supposed to come get us when that ghost appeared."

Michael jumped on the bed. "That's what I'm

tryna tell you! The ghost is here! She came to see us instead of Leo."

He pointed toward the window, where a shimmering figure could be seen wavering in and out of the moonlight. Harper squinted her eyes and beckoned to the figure. She reached over and grabbed Dayo's arm so that Dayo could see the ghost, too.

"Come on out where we can see you," she said.

Dayo jumped when she caught sight of the ghost, and a little *eek* squeaked out of her before she slapped a hand over her mouth.

Michael scrambled down to meet the materializing form of a little blond girl. She smiled shyly as Michael held out his hand for her. The two little ones came over to the bed together, hand in hand. Harper and Dayo stared in fascination.

"This is Holly. She's the one who was trying to talk to Leo. But she wasn't trying to scare him, she was trying to warn him," Michael explained

"Warn him about what?" Dayo asked.

"About the monsters," Holly replied, her big blue ghost eyes wide with fright. "They're coming."

"Who's coming?" Harper asked.

"Monsters," Holly whispered, looking quite terrified for a ghost. "They are the scariest monsters I've ever seen. They killed my parents."

"Oh, you poor thing," Dayo cried out. She reached over to hug the ghost, breaking contact with Harper. Dayo froze as the ghost disappeared from view. Sheepishly, she grabbed Harper's arm. "I forgot I can't see her unless I'm touching you."

Harper was staring at Holly. "How long have you been here?"

Holly shook her head. "I don't know. But it's been a long time, I think."

"Are your parents still with you?" Harper asked.

Holly looked like she was going to cry. "No," her little voice wavered. "The monsters ate their souls."

"Ate their souls?" Harper gasped as she immediately flashed back to the soul eater. "Can you describe the monsters to me?"

"They're really big, and really tall," she whispered. "Pale skin and claws, long claws. They have large mouths with lots of sharp teeth. But the scariest part is that they have no eyes."

That sounded exactly like the soul eater, but bigger. Yet the soul eater didn't kill anyone. At least, Harper didn't think so.

"Holly, can you tell me what happened to you and your family?"

The little ghost was silent for a long moment. "I remember we came for a vacation," she said. "Papa wanted to take me to Disney World, but Mama said it was too busy. She just wanted to relax on the beach. I was real excited because I had never been to the beach before."

Holly went quiet again. It was as if she was lost in memories.

"At first it was really nice here," she continued. "We were all so happy. But then I heard the drums."

Holly shuddered and shook her head. She flickered in and out as she began to wail. "It's all my fault! I shouldn't have followed the drums! It's all my fault!"

"Don't cry," Michael said, putting his arm around her. "It's not your fault."

Harper sighed. Holly looked like she was the same age as Michael. What a tragedy.

Both Dayo and Michael helped console the little ghost as Harper pondered Holly's story. Something was bothering her, and she needed to figure out what it was.

"Holly," Harper said gently, "can you tell us more about the monsters?"

Holly nodded. "They need human sacrifices. They go after people with bright auras, just like you and Michael."

"What about Leo?" Harper asked.

"Him, too, but his aura isn't quite as bright as

yours or Michael's," she said.

"Do I have a bright aura, too?" Dayo asked.

Holly cocked her head and looked at Dayo closely. "You have a pretty glow, but it isn't bright enough for the monsters."

Dayo looked both relieved and disappointed at once.

"Harper," Dayo said. "Didn't Rose say your aura was dimmed during the time you couldn't remember her?"

"Yeah, she did," Harper replied, saddened at the thought of her lost friend. After her horrible stay at Briarly, Harper had blocked out her abilities and forgotten Rose. During the year she lost her memory, Harper's usually bright aura had dimmed to almost nothing. "But I don't know how to do that myself."

"I think you need to try," Dayo said. "It's the only way for you and Michael to be safe."

"And you mustn't go out the night of Halloween!" Holly broke in. "That's when they're going hunting. And I think this year is special."

"Special? How?"

"The monsters—they're really excited. They're trying to break free of whatever holds them to this island."

"Do you know what that is, Holly?"

She shook her head. "But that's why they only want people with strong auras. It's supposed to help them escape."

"How do you know this?"

"I can hear the monsters talking to the person who is helping them."

"A live person?" Harper was stunned as Holly nodded.

"Do you know who it is?"

Holly shook her head. "I've been too scared to look. But it sounds like a woman."

"Why would anybody want to help these monsters escape?" Dayo asked.

"Maybe they were promised money or power," Harper said. "Or maybe they're just evil."

"But to let these terrible monsters out into the world?" Dayo shook her head. "Who can be that horrible?"

"We need to find out," Harper replied grimly. "Holly, do you know where you overheard them?"

"On the beach—there's a small cove that's close to Gorgon Grove. I heard them by accident once. I've been listening ever since."

"What were you doing at Gorgon Grove?" Dayo asked. "That place is horrible."

Holly was quiet. "It was where I died."

"Oh, I'm so sorry," Dayo said, her eyes filled with tears.

Harper really wanted to ask how it happened, but she knew it would be insensitive. Yet how could she know how to protect her brother if she didn't understand what the monsters had done before?

"Holly, is there anything you can tell us that would help?" Harper asked. "I'm worried about my brother, about what could happen to all of us."

Holly looked somberly at Michael and then looked back at Harper. "Whatever you do, don't go to Gorgon Grove."

It was a little past four a.m. when Michael finally went back to bed. Holly curled into a rocking chair next to him and seemed to fall asleep.

Dayo and Harper decided to talk in the morning.

Even after everyone else was fast asleep, Harper remained awake. She was agitated and distressed by all that she'd heard. When she finally closed her eyes, she found herself in the middle of a disturbing dream.

MONTGOMERY BENNINGTON'S ISLAND
April 28, 1912–Florida Keys

Harper knew she was dreaming because she was in the main cabin of a fancy yacht, staring at a group of people dressed like characters from the cast of an old period movie. The two men were wearing blazers and ties, and the three women were dressed in long flowy dresses and large brimmed hats, which struck her as ridiculous for a boat ride.

A tall handsome man wearing a captain's hat and a blue blazer with a funny-looking scarf tied to his neck shouted, "Land ho!" as he entered the cabin.

"Montgomery Bennington, you gave me a fright, I declare!" a pretty brunette woman said with a slight frown.

"I do beg your pardon, my dear Penelope," Montgomery said with a dashing bow. "I was just overcome with excitement to share my new discovery with my friends."

"Oh, have we arrived already?" Penelope asked.

"Almost," he answered. "My crew will let us know as soon as we are ready to disembark."

He crossed the room to join the two men standing by the bar area. His friends were a study in contrasts—tall and short, thin and chubby, dark and blond—but both were relieved to see Montgomery.

"Excellent timing, Monty," the dark-haired man drawled. "Roly and I have been dying for a cigar, but the ladies have been thoroughly cruel. Won't let us smoke in here, and won't let us leave them unattended. What's a bloke to do?"

"That was not well done of you to blame the ladies, Charles," the blond one named Roly said. He tried to smile at the women, but they ignored him.

"You can have your smoke when we land," Monty said. "And I'll entertain the ladies."

The women laughed. They were all very pretty.

"We are all so curious about your mystery island," Penelope said.

Before he could respond, there was a knock on the cabin door.

"Mr. Bennington, we've come into the lagoon as close as we can, and are ready to drop anchor," the crewman said as he stood outside the companionway door.

"You may proceed," Montgomery said with a languid wave.

"I say, Monty, how did you find this remote island of yours anyway?" Charles said as he peered out the cabin window. "It looks quite Robinson Crusoe."

"I drove by it a week ago when I was exploring. Didn't stop then. I figured that when you are discovering new islands, you might as well make a party out of it," Monty replied.

The women giggled again. "It's so funny to hear you say 'drove' instead of 'sailed,' as if you were driving a motorcar," Penelope said with a flirty smile. Meanwhile, her two redheaded friends batted their eyelashes at Charles, who looked uncomfortable.

Monty smiled. "Well, what else would you call it, my dear? This is a power yacht. It runs on petrol, just like that brand-new Mercer Raceabout your daddy bought you for your birthday."

"That's a mighty fine car, Miss Penelope, but not as fine as Monty's *Endeavor* here," Roly said with an ingratiating smile.

The women rolled their eyes at his pronouncement,

and Penelope raised an eyebrow in annoyance.

"Monty, will we be able to watch the eclipse from your island?" she asked. "It's supposed to be around six thirty tonight."

"Of course! We'll have the best view of anyone!" Monty replied.

"Perfect party-time activity," Charles cut in.

"But don't stare at the sun until the moon blocks it completely," Roly said. "Otherwise you'll damage your pretty eyes."

The women ignored him, instead giggling at Charles.

"Hey, Roly, I'm not sure the ladies know about your family's news," Monty said with a sly grin. "Apparently, Roly's parents have this property that they thought for years was worthless out in Ventura, California. And it just struck oil, and now they're richer than Croesus."

Harper didn't know what a Croesus was, but she could see that the women's reactions had now changed from contempt to fawning adoration. But she was also terribly bored with the dream. She wondered why she was stuck watching these awful people. She tried to wake herself up, but nothing was working. She peered out the port windows and saw that there was an island nearby. It had white-sand beaches, but it wasn't a lush, flower-laden para-dise. Far from it. The island had a twenty-foot bluff along a shore covered with the skeletal remains of white-bleached cedars and oak trees. But beyond the desolate beaches lay the thick jungle wilderness at the core of the island.

The boating party was now heading off, and Harper found herself pulled along as if by a large magnet.

The women complained as a chilly breeze blew their perfect hair into wild disarray.

"It's not very pretty, is it?" Penelope said. "I mean, it looks like a boneyard of trees."

For some reason, her words sent a shiver of fear down Harper's spine. This dream must be a memory of how the island was discovered.

Two crewmen had lowered a dinghy to take the party over to the island. The captain and first mate remained on board the yacht. Harper watched as the man named Monty helped Penelope and then her two friends onto the dinghy. The ladies shrieked as Charles jumped in, sending the dinghy rocking.

Instead of getting into the little boat, Monty rolled up his pants, took off his shoes and socks, and jumped into the lagoon. The water only came up to his knees.

Monty waded past the slow-moving dinghy, ignoring the cries of his other friend, Roly. Harper realized that she must be tied to Monty's memories, as she was suddenly pulled along with his form through the crystal-blue waters.

Suddenly a loud splash and cursing filled the air. Harper looked back to see Roly almost waist-deep in water.

"Curse you for being so tall!" Roland cried out as he waded forward.

Monty laughed and continued on. "You should have waited for the dinghy, Roly."

Monty was the first to reach the pure white sand. The beach stretched wide, framed on both sides by rock formations and skeletal trees. Large pieces of driftwood were strewn about like nature's art structures.

Monty's crewmen had already come to shore and set up an early picnic dinner on the beach. They prepared a simple spread of meats, cheeses, bread, and salads on a long wooden table and six folding chairs. Next to the table, several large blankets had been laid out.

"I do declare, this is the softest sand I've ever set foot on!" said one of the redheads.

"Oh, how lovely," Penelope said. "Why Monty,

your little island just might be a marvelous tourist attraction, with this soft, powdery sand. Key Largo doesn't even have any natural sand beaches."

"But we can go to Key West now, what with Henry Flagler's new railroad. They've got beaches there," her friend replied.

"I've been to Key West, and the beaches are not as nice as this," Penelope said. "They're all rocky and hard. This is like walking on powdered sugar. Monty, you said you always wanted to open up a top vacation resort. Why, you should open up a hotel right here."

Monty nodded, but Harper could see he was distracted. As the others sat down to eat, she followed Monty as he wandered into the thicket. For a moment she thought she could hear a faint drumming, and she felt a surge of panic. She wanted to warn him not to leave the beach, but he pushed his way through a tangle of overhanging tree limbs and walked farther into the jungle. The beach was shades of white and black, but the jungle was a rich visual feast. Colors here were brighter and the sounds clearer, but the air was muggy and thick.

Harper could hear the drums again. Staring at Monty, she knew he had to have heard them this time. He was standing still, listening intensely before finally moving again.

The dense jungle canopy above was alive with the sounds of life. The air buzzed with winged insects taking flight, and the ground moved with creepy-crawlies. Harper could see the remains of a dead bird completely covered with ants and other insects of the jungle. The only part uncovered was its yellow beak, which gaped open, a millipede crawling in as if heading home. Harper shuddered in disgust. All around them, the leaves trembled, as if there were invisible inhabitants watching and waiting.

Sweeping aside some protruding vines, Monty's hand caught within the sticky tendrils of a large cobweb. Pulling away, he shrank back from large spiders the size of his fists that crawled farther up their silky threads. Harper swallowed back a scream and then wondered if anyone would have even heard her.

The drums began to beat again, but how was that possible? She thought it was a deserted island, or was it? Could there be inhabitants? And if so, where were they? What were they doing? Were they watching them, waiting to spring a trap? Harper didn't want to continue. She wanted to wake up and get away from this nightmarish island, but she couldn't pull herself awake. She could only follow Monty as he stepped into a clearing and finally stopped. Before them stood a bizarre formation of palm trees that had twisted and bent themselves into unnatural positions, giving the appearance of Medusa's writhing serpentine hair. Harper recognized the trees immediately. This was Gorgon Grove.

The longer she stared at the hideous trees, the greater was the dread that rose within her. She sensed that they were trespassing on an ancient land. Something was out there—filled with malice that hit her like tidal waves. The trees themselves seemed to be warning them to leave, to run for their very lives. They shouldn't be here. The warped trunks seemed to shimmer and then undulate.

Peering closely, she noted that the largest of the trees had a blackened trunk, as if it had been struck many times by lightning. But on further inspection, Harper realized that the tree trunk was dotted with blood and what looked like human hair. There were even torn fingernails gouged into the bark. Repulsed, she took an involuntary step back.

Someone grabbed her arm, causing her to start violently and wake up.

NIGHTMARES AND MORE NIGHTMARES

Saturday, October 28—Later that morning

It took a long minute before Harper realized it was Dayo shaking her awake.

"Harper, you okay?" Dayo asked, a concerned frown on her face.

Rubbing her eyes, she nodded and sat up. "I had a bad nightmare."

"I'll say," Dayo said as she bounced off the bed. "You were breathing really loudly and shaking. What was it about?"

"I was in that horrible tree place."

Dayo shuddered. "That explains everything." She started changing into her clothes. "I'm done with the bathroom, so you should get ready now."

Harper stared blankly at Dayo, who shook her head and snorted.

"We're going to meet Olivia this morning, remember?"

Harper groaned and ran into the bathroom, chased by Dayo's chuckles.

At nine a.m. sharp, Harper, Dayo, Leo, and Michael were riding in a white hotel van through the winding roads of the resort grounds. Dayo was all about punctuality.

"So, what happened last night, Leo?" Harper said. "Why didn't you wake us?"

Leo looked puzzled. "It didn't come last night," he said. "And I slept well last night, too."

"No, she just visited me instead," Michael said.

Leo looked upset. "No . . . not again. What does it want? How can we make it go away?"

"Don't worry, Leo," Harper said. "She's just a little lost ghost baby. We're gonna help her find her way back to where she belongs."

"Why would you help a ghost? You're supposed to get rid of it!"

"This is how, dummy," Harper rolled her eyes.

"How do I know this is going to work?"

"She's not bothering you, right?"

Leo had no response.

"Aren't you going to thank us?" Harper said.

"Why?" Leo snapped. "You're the reason I got like this."

Harper raised an eyebrow.

"I mean, thank you," he said grudgingly.

"Well, you also have to promise never to pull another prank on us ever again," Harper said.

"Yeah, no pranks, you big meanie!" Michael said.

Leo was quiet for a long moment.

"Then I'm gonna tell that little ghost girl to keep haunting you . . . ," Harper said.

"Okay! I promise never to prank you guys again."

The cousins shook on their agreement just as the van reached a large house overlooking a secluded beach cove. Something about the area had Harper buzzing with alarm.

As they approached the house, Olivia came running out of the front door, followed by a tall woman with dark brown hair pulled into a tight bun. She was wearing white slacks and a navy vest belted at the waist. Her lips were smiling even though her eyes were not.

"Hi, guys, this is my mom! She wanted to meet you all before she went into the office," Olivia said. She quickly introduced everyone and ended with Leo. "You remember Leo, right?"

"Yes, of course," Mrs. Bennington said with a wide smile. "Your parents were the best thing to happen to our resort." Her eyes sized up everyone else and then turned back to her daughter. "So, how are all of you enjoying the island?"

"It's beautiful," Dayo said.

"Yeah, and the food is the bestest," Michael said, holding two thumbs up.

Mrs. Bennington leaned down with a genuine smile to caress Michael's cheek. "I'm so glad. We hire the best chefs in the business. Like your uncle."

Straightening up, she pulled out her car keys and put on her sunglasses. "Well, it was very nice to meet you all," she said with a polite smile. "Please enjoy yourselves. And Olivia, don't forget, I want you at the hotel for dinner with the Garlands."

Olivia nodded and gave her mother a kiss on the cheek. They all watched as Mrs. Bennington got into a silver Mercedes-Benz and drove off.

Olivia turned to the kids with a bright smile. "Are you guys hungry? My chef made lots of food for us."

They followed her to the back of the house, where a large buffet table had been set with platters of food. Pancakes, crepes, and waffles, as well as eggs, bacon, and hash browns were piled up, along with a mound of fresh fruit.

As the others loaded up their plates, Harper grabbed two of her own, filling one with pancakes and fruit and the other one with eggs, bacon, and potatoes.

Olivia started giggling. "Do you always eat from two plates?"

"I don't like different types of food touching each other," Harper explained.

"But it's all breakfast foods," Olivia said.

"Sweet and savory shouldn't mix."

Dayo rolled her eyes. "Harper, you could always just eat from one plate at a time."

"But that would be a waste," Harper said. "I want to eat them all together."

"Then it shouldn't matter if they touch," Olivia laughed.

"Ew, gross," Harper said. She took a big bite of her eggs and bacon and chased it with a maple syrup–covered pancake.

After breakfast, they played games and then changed into swimming gear before the snorkeling instructor arrived.

The instructor, Tomas, was a dark-skinned young guy with a dazzling smile and eyes that were full of mischief. He spoke with a lilting accent and said he was from Saint Lucia. They all liked him immediately.

"Mrs. Bennington sent over these rash-guard shirts from the store for you all. They are yours to keep, so put them on now. They will prevent you from getting sunburned," Tomas said. He then gave them all flotation devices that wrapped around their waists, except for Michael, who got a flotation vest instead.

"But I'm a good swimmer!" Michael whined.

"And I believe you," Tomas said. "But sometimes the undercurrent can get tricky, and even strong swimmers could get pulled under. So, it would be better to be safe than turn into a mermaid, right, little man?"

"How do you turn into a mermaid?"

"Well, you take in too much water and can't come back to land," Tomas said as he put the vest on Michael. "But you would miss land too much—your friends and family and ice cream. You can't eat ice cream if you're a mermaid."

"I love ice cream," Michael said.

"Oh, I see. You love it more than your family?" Harper asked jokingly.

Michael laughed. "No, silly."

They all lined up for their snorkeling gear and listened as Tomas told them where they could and couldn't go. "You must stay in the cove. You see the rope with all the colorful buoys? Do not pass that rope, got it?"

Harper did a thumbs-up as she put on the full face mask. The rope was at the mouth of the cove, which led into the ocean. The difference in the waves within the cove and outside the cove was enough to persuade Harper to avoid the rope area.

She followed the others into the shallows, and they waded up to their hips before they all put their faces into the water. Immediately she was transported into another world. Tiny colorful fish fluttered by her nose as she moved through the crystal-blue water. She could see Tomas swimming next to Michael, keeping him close by his side. Knowing her brother was safe, Harper began to explore.

Dayo and Olivia were up ahead. They turned to her and motioned for her to come. Harper kicked her fins to follow them, then she caught a quick movement in the corner of her eye. It was an octopus. Fascinated, she followed it as it slunk along the sandy floor, using its long tentacles to grab on to rocks and pull itself forward. Harper was right behind the octopus when it suddenly jerked forward and propelled itself quickly through the water, launching itself like a bullet. Harper wondered what had happened, and then she noticed the water turning dark around her.

Something pale glimmered in the water—she turned toward it and then reeled back aghast. It was a dead body, held down in the water with heavy rocks. She immediately swam away, but something grabbed her by the ankle. She stared in horror at the pale dead hand that was now holding her tight. Harper kicked wildly, trying to shake the hand off. Instead, the body came loose from the rocks and a slew of corpses erupted from the bottom of the sea. Screaming inside her face mask, Harper kicked violently at the dead thing and swam for her life.

She broke the surface of the water and pulled off her mask, gasping for air, as Leo stared back at her.

"Harper, you're beyond the cove," he said. "We've got to go back."

"I saw something," she wheezed. She pointed down.

Leo immediately dove below but came right back up. "There's nothing there."

Harper didn't argue. She just wanted to get away as quickly as possible. She followed Leo back to the rope and into the safety of the cove.

After another spectacular lunch and an afternoon filled with more fun activities, they left to go home before dinner. Olivia told them that there would be more activities at the hotel the next day and made plans to meet them there.

But Harper couldn't shake the image of those dead bodies. Back at the house, Harper pulled Dayo aside to tell her what happened. Horrified by the vision, the girls went on Aunt Caroline's computer to do more research.

"Okay, so you know all about Montgomery Bennington and how he found the island and made all these hotels," Dayo said. "What we don't know are all the juicy backstories."

Over the years, Razu Island had been known for mysterious disappearances. When the resort was popular, the disappearances were not so noticeable, but after Monty's death, the hotel didn't attract as many tourists. For a small island with a population of no more than a thousand locals, the disappearances began to look suspicious.

It was during Monty's grandson's ownership that the real tragedy occurred. Todd Bennington inherited the hotel chain at the age of twenty. For the first few years of Todd's reign, there were no mysterious disappearances or deaths. But then tragedy struck. Sixteen people were murdered, including a young family. Their bodies were hideously dismembered and left at Gorgon Grove. The worst part was the death of a young child.

While the hotel's reputation suffered, Todd had his own tragedies. The year after the murders, the resort was closed and Todd's first son, born that spring, died of unknown causes. The following year, he caused a scandal by deserting his pregnant wife, Clarissa, and disappearing.

Clarissa Bennington came from a small town in Florida to work as a waitress in the hotel restaurant. It caused a scandal when Todd married her. The board of directors called her a gold digger and tried to ignore her existence. Ironically, it was the same board of directors who praised her when she was able to make the hotel chain successful again.

"Wow, this place is a mess," Dayo said, rubbing her eyes. "Poor Olivia. She had it real rough. But you gotta respect Olivia's mom for saving this place."

"I don't think I like her," Harper said abruptly. "She gives me the creeps."

"That's not nice to say about Olivia's mom," Dayo said. "I mean, she is kind of cold, but I'm sure she's a good mom."

"Just because you're a good mom doesn't make you a good person," Harper said.

"Yeah, I hear you," Dayo said. "So, the murderers have to be the monsters, right?"

"Yep." Harper grabbed her phone to call her grandma. The call went straight to voice mail. Harper sighed and got back on the computer and wrote up a long message in an email to her grandmother.

"Well, all we can do is wait," she said.

"I hope she gets back to you sooner than she usually does," Dayo said.

"I'll call my aunt if she doesn't respond," Harper said. She shuddered as she thought of the dead bodies in the water. "In fact, I'll call her right away."

THE TREES OF GORGON GROVE

Sunday, October 29

The next day Harper's mom took Kelly, Harper, Dayo, and Michael to the little town not far from the resort. Leo stayed home to play video games. The bus drove them to a local market crowded with tourists looking at pink flamingo earrings and seashell souvenirs.

Yuna and Kelly stopped at a jewelry stall, while Harper and Dayo followed Michael as they wandered between the narrow aisles crowded with shoppers. He made a beeline for a stand filled with colorful wooden toy boats. He picked up a sturdy-looking red-and-blue tugboat, pretending it was fighting large tidal waves. A little girl with curly blond hair came over to watch him.

"That's my favorite," she said.

"Me too," Michael replied.

"Look, it even has a real propeller, and towlines to tow a bigger boat. Here, like this." The girl grabbed a large freight ship and attached it to the end of the tugboat.

"Cool!" Michael said. "I'm gonna ask my Mom if I can have this."

"That's a very good choice," the girl said seriously. Harper smothered a laugh. The little girl couldn't have been older than Michael, and yet she had the practiced assurance of an experienced salesperson.

"I'm almost six. How old are you?" she asked.

"I'm five," Michael said. "I like chocolate ice cream."

"Me too!"

They both beamed at each other and giggled.

"I'm Kayla. What's your name?"

"Michael," he replied. "You're so lucky to have all these boats."

"My dad makes them, so I have lots," she said. She then turned to her mom and yelled, "Mommy, this little boy wants to buy the tugboat."

Her mother came over, a smile creasing her plump round face. "Well, it seems like he has excellent taste, then," she said. "My husband carves them by hand, and the tugboats are our top sellers. Hard to keep in stock."

The woman winked cheerfully at Harper. Suddenly, she paled and stood staring at a young teenage boy who'd walked in with his family. Harper turned to look also. He was a fairly nondescript teen with dirty-blond hair and a sullen expression on his face, following his parents around and clearly unhappy. The only thing Harper noticed that was unusual was that the boy had a strange triangular bruise on his neck right under his chin and close to his right ear.

The parents approached the owner to ask a question, but the owner couldn't help staring. Then she tore her gaze away and abruptly announced that the stall was closing.

Harper wanted to purchase the boat, but the woman waved her away, telling her to keep the boat. Then she shooed everyone out and pulled her curtain closed.

Harper couldn't understand what had spooked the woman so badly. But her eyes were drawn once again to the sullen teenager as he slouched on a bench outside.

The sun was shining brightly on his face, making the bruise vivid. It looked like a claw mark.

Something about the mark made Harper think of the monsters that the little ghost girl had been talking about. What did the mark mean? Was he in danger? She walked over to ask him.

"Hey, what happened to your neck?" she asked.

He looked up at her in surprise and then shrugged. "I just woke up this morning with it. I have no idea how I got it except I had a really bad nightmare. Maybe I hit myself with something, I don't know."

"What kind of nightmare?" Harper asked.

"None of your business, nosy," he snapped. He got up to his feet and stalked off.

Dayo came over, holding Michael's hand. "What was that about?"

"I don't know," Harper said. "But it's related somehow. I can feel it."

Someone shouted their names. When they turned to see who it was, Kelly came over with a cheerful grin. "Come on, guys, there's a Smoothie Hut around the corner. Let's go get some tropical fruit drinks."

Michael whooped with joy and happily held Kelly's hand to run ahead.

"You know, the beach sure makes Kelly happy," Dayo said.

"You mean she acts more human?" Harper asked.

"I heard that!" Kelly yelled at them.

Soon after, they headed back to the house, and Yuna took Michael to his watersport class, while Harper and Dayo huddled together in the dining room over milk and a plate of pastries.

"I think we have to go to Gorgon Grove," Harper said. "I feel like the answer is there."

Dayo shuddered. "Do we have to? That place gives me the creeps. Can't we try your grandma again?"

"I've tried twice. Grandma's not answering, and neither is my aunt Youjin," Harper said. "Service is so bad here on the island. You don't have to go if you don't want to."

"Oh yes I do," Dayo said. "If you're going, I'm going."

"Going where?" Leo asked as he grabbed a pastry.

"Gorgon Grove," Dayo replied. "Do you know how we can get there?"

Leo nodded. "There's a tour that leaves this afternoon, and one of the stops is the grove."

"Perfect," Harper said. "Where do we get it?"

"I'll take you," Leo said. "I haven't done the tour in a while. It might be fun."

Harper made a face at Dayo, but Leo didn't see it.

Later that afternoon, the three of them walked over to the hotel and took the shuttle bus tour. The first stop was a botanical garden. Harper walked impatiently through the vivid and lush beauty of the garden, but Dayo and Leo seemed to enjoy the tour. Colorful birds flew in and out of the foliage.

Finally, the tour took them to Gorgon Grove. The guide began his talk with a history of the Bennington family and the importance of the trees. When developers asked if they could chop down the grove because it was such an eyesore, Monty Bennington refused. The tour guide said it was because Bennington was a passionate environmentalist.

Harper and Dayo looked at each other and simultaneously rolled their eyes. One woman standing next to them shuddered. "I think they are hideous and frightening," she said loudly. "If it was me, I would have chopped them down years ago."

"Especially after those awful murders," another woman chimed in. "What's the real story about them anyway?"

The tour guide ignored the question and began to lead them to the nearby lagoon, expounding on the different types of trees and flowers and other terribly boring stuff. Suddenly, Harper heard what sounded like the faint beat of drums. Without telling Dayo, Harper walked away from the tour, following the drums, until she reached one particularly large, grotesque tree. She recognized the tree from her previous nightmare vision. She stared at the blackened lightning scorches on the trunk, which seemed to grow in size until it became the only thing she could see. Then, someone grabbed her arm. As she whirled around, she realized that she was in Monty's body.

THE ISLAND OF
MONSTERS
April 28, 1912—Florida Keys

S he gasped, and it sounded like a man's voice.
She could hear his thoughts and feel his emotions. Harper was back in the dream, but not as an
observer. She was now Montgomery Bennington.
This had never happened to her before. She wondered if this was a sign of her growing abilities, but
she would think about it later. Clearly, she was meant
to learn something more from Bennington.

"Sorry about that, old man. Didn't mean to give
you a fright." Charles's voice came as if from a distance. "I say, these are the most bizarre trees I've
ever seen. No wonder you look so scared." Charles let
out a brash laugh.

Monty shuddered. He wanted to slap a hand over his friend's mouth and beg him to be quiet. Death lay beyond the trees—Monty was certain of that. It was ancient and evil. Waiting. Watching them.

"I hate to be a pain, but the ladies are getting put out by your continued absence."

Monty tried to laugh, but it sounded more like a croak. His voice seemed hoarse, as if something was lodged in his throat. "We'd best return, then."

Without a backward glance, he hastened away. He hadn't gone far when he turned to see that Charles was not behind him. He whirled around, calling Charles's name sharply.

"Be right there," Charles said. "Nature calls."

A deep foreboding gripped him. "Charles, perhaps you should go back to the boat?"

"Don't be ridiculous, I'll only be a minute—you go on ahead."

Monty wanted to run back and pull his friend away, but the dread forced him toward the beach. He told himself not to be paranoid. It was just a bunch of trees. Nothing to be frightened about. By the time he reached the picnic blankets, he had convinced himself that he'd overreacted.

"Where's Charles?" one of the redheads asked. He could never remember their names.

"Oh, he'll be along shortly," Monty said.

"A man's gotta do what a man's gotta do," Roland said.

Penelope rolled her eyes as redheaded wonders number one and two giggled. Monty could feel the beginnings of a headache settle in behind his eyeballs.

He went over to the picnic table and quickly made himself a sandwich and tore into it, as if the act of chewing would resolve his headache. He paid no attention to the idle chatter. Instead, he was tuned to the jungle behind him, waiting for the sound of Charles's return. The dread was back, filling his stomach so that every mouthful dropped like lead pellets into a churning whirlpool. He threw down his sandwich.

"Come on, Charles, where the heck are you?" he whispered to himself. But the dread told him that his friend would not be returning.

"He's taking an awfully long time," Roland said as he rose to his feet to come and stand by Monty's side. "Perhaps the long boat ride didn't agree with him."

"Poor thing, do you think he's sick out there?" Penelope asked.

Someone giggled.

"Maybe one of y'all should go hold a bucket for him," one of the other girls said.

"Would you be quiet?!" Monty yelled, causing an affronted silence. "He's been too long. We should go after him."

Yet he found it difficult to move his feet. The dread had seeped down from his stomach and into his lower limbs. He feared his legs would shake and he would fall ignominiously in front of the others.

Roland marched forward. "Never fear, I'll go after him, old chap," he said. "You stay here with the ladies."

Monty watched as Roland's short portly shape disappeared into the jungle, the lush green plants and vines swallowing up his form, leaving no evidence of his passing behind. The faint sound of drumming filled Monty's ears again.

"Did you hear that?" he whispered to the women.

Penelope and her friends exchanged significant looks before gazing back at him. "Hear what?" Penelope asked.

"That drumming sound! There it goes again. Can't you hear it now?"

The women looked at each other.

"We don't hear anything but the ocean," one of the redheads replied.

Monty turned away, clutching at his hair. How could it be that they could not hear what was so clear in his head? First Charles, and now Roland. The jungle had taken his two best friends, and he was too afraid to do anything about it. He paced back and forth, beating his fist into his hand as he argued with himself. Minutes passed with agonizing slowness. And still they did not return.

"Monty, if they don't come back soon, they're going to miss the eclipse," Penelope said. "I think it's starting." She pointed to the horizon, where the sky was turning dark as night.

Monty swore furiously under his breath.

"Gabriel, bring me my Winchester!" Monty yelled to one of his two crewmen. Gabriel ran to the dinghy and returned with a long bundle. He untied it to reveal a Winchester Model 1903 semiautomatic rifle and a box of .22 Winchester Automatic cartridges.

"Monty, what are you doing?" Penelope asked.

Ignoring her, he loaded his rifle and began to walk away. "Gabriel, you come with me. Jonah, take the ladies back to the boat, and tell the captain to be ready to set sail."

"Monty, surely you're overreacting!" Penelope yelled. "Don't be silly. They are probably pulling a prank on you!"

Monty turned briefly to face her and tried to smile but failed. "I dearly hope you're right," he said. Turning away, he headed toward the jungle. The heavy weight of the Winchester in his arms gave him false comfort, steadying him on his feet. Twisted limbs seemed to dip down ominously from their treetops as he brushed past a curtain of leafy vines. Whatever warmth had been on the beach seemed to be sucked out of the very air he breathed. Behind him, Gabriel's sturdy steps sounded as they headed deeper into the island.

This time, the jungle all around him was motionless, silent but for their own passage and the faint beating of the drums. Not even the drone of a mosquito could be heard. It bothered him. Something was very off. He gazed down at the jungle floor, which had previously been teeming with insects. Now, none could be found.

The terrible drumming filled his ears, louder than ever before. With every step, the drums sent his heart into rapid palpitations. He was finding it harder and harder to breathe. What was the madness that this island had infected him with? He began to loathe the island. Had it lured him in only to drive him mad? Above him, the sky grew progressively darker.

"Mr. Bennington, are there natives on this island?" Gabriel asked.

Monty reeled around in relief. "You hear them, too? Thank the Lord, I thought I was going mad!"

Suddenly, the other man let out a loud gasp and crossed himself. *"Madre de Dios!"*

Monty was afraid to turn around, transfixed by the growing horror on Gabriel's face. The man stumbled, fell, and began to scream. Monty felt a presence pass right by him—a creature that blotted out the sky. But it was as if he was frozen in place, paralyzed in both mind and body. He could see it heading straight for Gabriel, but he couldn't shout out a warning. His voice had disappeared. A blur of movement flung itself at his crewman, even as the man stared off in a different direction. The creature was pale. A large sinewy claw grasped the screaming man by his leg and began dragging him away.

Gabriel was screaming, twisting and turning on the ground as he fought helplessly against the creature. "What is it? I can't see it! I can't see it! Help me! Please, help me! I don't want to die!" His fingers clawed at the ground, trying to grab for anything to save himself. He flung out an entreating hand toward Monty, his eyes desperate with terror as he screamed one final time.

All this imprinted into Monty's memory.

Gabriel's cries faded away, muffled by the jungle

as his body disappeared. Monty let out a shuddering breath. The paralysis that had gripped him passed, causing him to stagger and fall to the ground. He had to get away before it came back, but his legs betrayed him. Why couldn't Gabriel see the creature that had attacked him? What had he been staring at that had scared him so badly? Monty turned his head slowly, toward the spot Gabriel had been facing. There, propped up against the Medusa-like trees, were Charles and Roland, sitting with their eyes closed, as if napping. Except that their guts had been torn out and their empty rib cages peered through their gored abdomens.

A surge of vomit poured out of Monty as he lay retching in the tall grass. He began to crawl away, choking back hysterical sobs, willing his legs to stand.

"For God's sake, Monty, what on earth are you doing?"

He looked up, his mind not comprehending the sight of the three women before him. They were holding lanterns, for the area had become almost completely dark.

"We sent Jonah after you but can't seem to find him. The eclipse has started. We must return immediately to the beach if we are to catch the totality," Penelope said.

Monty stared, horrified. Why were they there? They should have been safe on the boat. "You need to get out of here," he said. "You need to run!"

"Have you lost your mind?" Penelope asked. She knelt down and placed a cool hand on his forehead. "Monty, honestly, I think you must be ill or coming down with something."

"Run," he whispered. "Run. Run."

One of the women began to scream. The other moaned Charles's name over and over.

"Don't look!" Monty grabbed Penelope's hand. "You don't want to see it."

Fear and alarm creased Penelope's beautiful face as she stared back at him. He could see her dawning realization that something was terribly wrong.

At that moment, bloodcurdling screams exploded beside them.

Penelope whimpered as she looked up. "What's happening?"

Her two redheaded friends were surrounded by several of the demon-like monsters. It was as if the monsters were toying with them, flinging them around like rag dolls, their bodies contorting wildly as they shrieked. The women fell to the ground with terrible thuds before being dragged away through the tall grass. Penelope leaped forward and tried to grab one of her friends' hands. Monty shot to his feet, catching Penelope's arm and covering her mouth. He could still glimpse the creatures as they dragged the redheads away.

"Don't make a sound. Run away, quietly," he whispered.

Releasing her, he pushed Penelope toward the safety of the beach when she suddenly screamed as if her heart had been torn out of her chest. Monty turned to see a creature heading back toward them. He shoved Penelope fiercely. "For God's sake, woman, run for your life!"

She took off in a crazy dash for safety, holding her lantern high. The very air around them seemed to try to stop their progress as vines tore at their clothes and roots tripped their feet. The jungle shifted as they ran. Finally, they reached soft sands and navigated around large, tangled pieces of driftwood. Penelope had pulled far ahead of him and was splashing in the water toward the boat, when Monty felt the creature catch up to him. He was thrown high in the air and dropped down again into the sand, face-first. He flung himself over and stared up into the face of a demon. Pale leatherlike skin pulled tight as the creature's fleshy mouth gaped open, highlighting sharp fangs that gleamed in the light. But where its eyes should have been there were none, only two slits for nostrils.

"Please don't kill me! Dear God, don't kill me!" Monty scrambled to his knees, cringing. Something primitive within him caused him to genuflect before it. He remained bowed for several long moments. When nothing happened, he peered up cautiously.

The creature had stopped and was sniffing him all over with almost a quizzical expression. Above its head, Monty could see that the sun was totally eclipsed by the moon. But he could not appreciate it. He cringed as the monster placed a long claw upon his head. Suddenly, he was overwhelmed with images of an ancient time and a great golden temple—a vast land with millions of people worshipping statues that looked like the creature before him. Then the image of a chanting priest in a long white-and-gold robe, and a human sacrifice left in shackles before the altar.

"You are ancient gods. You need sacrifices. I'll bring them to you! I'll be your priest. I'll bring you many, many sacrifices, if only you will let me go!" Monty pleaded.

Images flooded his mind again, blood and

violence and an overwhelming hunger. Monty gripped his head in agony and screamed—his brain throbbing from the creature's communications. He saw a holy woman in red, fighting the creatures with a staff and the crashing of cymbals. Their temples were destroyed, and the once-powerful gods vanished from the land of people. Only on this one island could they enter the human world, and not for long.

Monty felt something akin to malevolent satisfaction in the thoughts of the creature before him. The power of the total eclipse gave them the chance to walk the earth again, and he was the first human to communicate with them—the first to offer them the old ways. The creature reached down, caressing Monty's neck with the tip of one blackened claw. He felt a searing pain that faded into a dull throb. And then the creature disappeared, and Monty fell back into the sand.

He could hear Penelope screaming his name from far away, but he didn't know why. Drool dripped down his lips and chin, pooling in his sandy collar. He was aware of the sky lightening above him and the sun's rays glistening over the blue of the water. He could hear each individual wave that crested nearby.

Arms lifted him up, and he peered around to find the captain and his first mate at his side, leading him gently back to the dinghy.

"What happened? Am I dreaming?" he asked.

"No, Mr. Bennington. We don't know what happened. You went flying through the air and took a bad fall before you fainted. That's when we reached you," the captain said as he and the first mate rowed the dinghy. "But you're safe now."

On board the *Endeavor*, Monty sat in the cabin across from Penelope, both wrapped in blankets as they sped back to civilization. He could hear the argument between Penelope and the captain. She'd refused to let them search for the others, screaming that they were all dead and ordering the captain to take them home.

Monty could hear her weeping softly, but he had no desire to console her. He stared blindly into space, trying desperately to forget the images the creature had left in his brain.

"Razu." He muttered the strange name that the creature had imprinted in his brain. "Razu Island." He touched a hand to his neck and felt the triangular raised mark of the creature on his skin. Suddenly he began to laugh. Penelope glared at him in disgust, but he couldn't stop. Tears rolled down his face as he laughed with hysterical madness.

They were safely away, heading home.

But Monty knew that he would never be free.

THE RAZU

Sunday, October 29—Late afternoon

She could hear someone calling her name, and then someone poked at her. She blinked and gradually focused on Dayo's and Leo's worried expressions.

"Harper, you were standing there staring at nothing for such a long time," Leo said. "You weren't even blinking. How's that even possible?"

Dayo ignored him and put an arm around her friend. "You okay? You had another vision?"

Harper nodded. She could feel her heart pounding like a frightened bird in her chest. The vision was too intense, too frightening. She started crying.

"I know what the monsters are," she said, her voice raspy with fear.

"Monsters? What is she talking about?" Leo asked.

"They're called Razu," she continued. "This is really bad. We have to get help."

Leo backed away. "We have to get back on the bus right now."

Harper could see the fear on her cousin's face. She looked at Dayo and said, "I'll tell you on the bus."

They sat in the rear of the bus. Leo stayed in the front, allowing Harper to tell Dayo everything she'd learned.

When she was inside Monty's memories, she saw what the monsters had shared with him—their history. They were once hailed as living gods. Four of them. They had more human forms back then, until the lust for human blood and flesh changed them into grotesque monsters. Demons. They enslaved an entire population, but then they became gluttonous and decimated all the humans. The Razu left their land, seeking new slaves, and would lay waste to whole tribes. Until one day they slaughtered an entire village and fell into a deep sleep in the forest that would become Gorgon Grove. A female shaman, who had been tracking them, found the Razu in a deep sleep. By herself, she could not kill them all, and she could not kill one without waking the others. So, she captured them and imprisoned them in the spiritual world. The location where this occurred was then separated from the coastland and launched into the sea as an island, so that no human could ever accidentally release the monsters. The Razu didn't know how she captured them, but they'd been seeking revenge for centuries, desperate to finally escape and walk the earth once more.

The soul eater that had taken Rose was a much smaller and weaker manifestation of the Razu that they projected into the human world to collect souls. On the island, so close to where they were imprisoned, they could manifest into larger, more deadly versions of themselves. But here they preyed only on those humans with strong auras. One human soul with a strong aura was equal to twenty without.

But the more souls they collected, the more power they had. Soon, Harper feared, they could break through the binding and enter the world once and for all, desperately hungry for blood and flesh.

"What can we do?" Dayo's eyes were wide with fright.

"I have to reach my grandmother."

Back at the house, Harper tried again to call her grandmother and then her aunt, but no luck.

"I'm going to have to call a spiritual adviser,"

Harper said. "Hopefully, there is one nearby that can help me."

From her suitcase, Harper took out three brass bowls, the bells Wisdom and Truth, and her *mudang* bells. She sat down on the floor and unpacked a stack of neatly folded crisp white paper in a ziplock bag, a large container of sea salt, and a plastic bottle filled with holy water. Her parents hadn't been happy when Harper had to check her bag at the airport due to the holy water. But they hadn't argued about it. The only thing she couldn't bring was her lighter or even a book of matches.

"I don't have matches for the paper," Harper said. "But I bet my aunt has some in the kitchen."

"Your uncle is down there right now baking," Dayo said.

"Rats," Harper said. "Okay, so we will do it without the purification step."

She used her *mudang* bells to summon a spirit, but no one came except Holly, who watched in wide-eyed fascination. Harper kept trying, but still nothing. It was as if there were no spirits in the area, except for Holly.

"What are you doing?" Holly asked.

"I'm trying to call a spiritual adviser," Harper said.

"What's a spiritual adviser?" Holly asked.

"A ghost who's been here for a long time," Harper said. "But I can't reach anyone."

"That's because there aren't any," Holly said. "I'm the only one on the entire island."

Harper dropped her bells with loud clangs. "None?" she asked.

Holly shook her head.

"Of course," Harper said grimly. "They're soul eaters."

"What do we do now?" Dayo asked.

"I'll call my aunt!" Harper said. She dialed the number, but it kept going to voice mail. She left a message with her aunt to have her grandmother call her, and then she called her mother.

"What's the matter, Harper?" Yuna asked.

"Mom, I tried to reach Auntie Youjin to see if she could get Grandma for me," Harper said, "but no one is answering."

"That's because they're all at the hospital," Yuna replied. "She's been having the longest labor ever. What's the matter?"

Harper sighed. She'd forgotten all about the baby.

"Nothing. I just wanted to ask Grandma a question, that's all," she said.

"Well, hopefully I'll hear from Auntie Youjin

soon, but first babies can take a long time to deliver," Yuna replied. "Michael is almost done with his camp, and we'll be back at the house in time for dinner."

Harper turned to Dayo with a helpless expression. "I just don't know what to do now," she said.

"Don't worry," Dayo said with a bright smile. "I'm sure she'll call back soon."

Harper really hoped so, too.

A MONSTER COMES CALLING

Sunday, October 29—Late night

Harper heard a sharp cry. She got out of bed and walked over to the connecting door to peer in at Michael. Moonlight streamed in through the shades of the large window overlooking the beach, illuminating the room clearly. He was feverishly twisting within a tangle of sheets, moaning and whimpering. Dayo sat up in the other bed, rubbing her eyes. She turned on the light between their two beds.

"Poor baby," she said. "Sounds like a bad nightmare."

Harper walked over and tried to shake her brother gently awake. "Michael, wake up."

It took him a while to come out of the nightmare,

his body still locked in a battle with his mind, eyeballs rolling madly behind tightly shut eyelids. Finally, he woke up and dove into Harper's arms, hugging her fiercely. He was trembling badly, mumbling about monsters and ghosts.

"You're safe. It's just a dream," she said. She rubbed his back until his sobs stopped and he calmed down. Tucking him in, she noticed a red triangular mark on the right side of his neck, underneath his jawline.

Harper froze in concern. It was the same mark that the teenage boy had earlier that day. She rubbed gently at the small mark.

"Ouch! That hurts!" he cried out, shoving her hand away.

Dayo came over to peer at the mark also.

"How'd you get this?" Harper asked.

Michael shuddered as he placed a hand over the mark. "In my dream, the monster stabbed me right here with its claw." He looked at her with tears in his eyes. "Do you think it was real?"

"No way," Harper said. "Maybe you poked yourself there as you were flailing around like a wild thing. There's no such thing as monsters," Harper lied, not wanting her brother to be scared.

Michael was quiet, and he looked up at her with

wide, frightened eyes. "People say there's no such thing as ghosts also."

"Ghosts are the souls of people who have died," Harper replied. "They were real. Their souls are real. But monsters? There aren't any monsters here."

"It looked real. I'm scared—I don't want to stay here no more. I want to go home!" Michael said, beginning to cry again. "I want Mommy."

Harper carried him to her parents' room. Yuna opened the door before she could even knock, immediately gathering Michael up into a tight hug.

"Go to bed, sweetie. I'll take care of him now," Yuna said. She caressed Harper's cheek before heading back in.

Harper returned to her room and saw that Dayo had fallen back asleep. The mark on her brother's neck had really scared her. It was as if he'd been marked by the Razu. She pulled out her shaman bag and headed for the stairs. This time she needed to do the purification ritual, and she needed matches. She knew there had to be some in the kitchen.

She crept downstairs, making her way by the slivered moonbeams that cut through the darkness. As she pondered where in the kitchen her aunt would keep matches, a voice spoke from behind her, making her jump.

"Watcha looking for?"

Harper turned to see Holly perched on the counter. She was swinging her legs happily, as if she was waiting for someone to serve her a delicious meal.

"I'm looking for matches," Harper said. "Do you think you know where they are?"

Holly nodded. "I saw your uncle put them in that cabinet next to the refrigerator. He was barbecuing on the grill out there."

Harper opened the cabinet and found a large box of kitchen matches on the top shelf.

"I miss hamburgers," Holly said wistfully.

She looked so sad that Harper wished she could somehow make her a hamburger and then realized how impossible that was.

"I'm sorry, Holly."

"It's all right. I miss my mom and dad the most," she said, "and I was thinking that maybe you could help me get back to them."

Harper sat on the other side of the counter, facing Holly. "I'd love to help you," she said. "Are you ready to talk about what happened?"

The little ghost nodded. "I remember that night. It was all my fault."

Holly's eyes seemed far away, lost in a memory.

"I was sleeping when I heard the drumming. I

just had to follow it," Holly said. "It led me all the way to the scary trees. But there were already a lot of people there. They all had marks on their necks, just like your brother has. I didn't know if they were dead or just sleeping, but they were all lying on the ground, all around the trees. And then I saw them. I was screaming. My parents. They must have been trying to find me."

Holly began flickering in and out as she became more distressed. "They couldn't see the monsters, but I could. I saw them kill my parents. I tried to run away, but I fell and hit my head. When I woke up, I was like this and the monsters were sucking the souls of the people into their mouths. I just ran away. I went back to our hotel room, because I thought maybe I would wake up and it was all just a nightmare. But it wasn't."

"Holly, did you see a light from the sky? Something that might have pulled at you?"

She nodded. "Yes, but it was too close to where the monsters were." Holly looked up hopefully. "Can you find that light for me again? It felt peaceful. I wouldn't be lonely anymore."

Harper felt the prick of tears in her eyes as she thought of Rose. "Yes. I have a good friend up there who would be happy to meet you. I'll ask my grandma.

She'll know what to do. But please do me a favor and watch over Michael for me until then, okay?"

Holly smiled wide and glowed brightly with happiness. "Okay! I won't let the monsters get him, I promise."

Harper stepped out onto the patio and took out her container of salt. She shook out a large circle and sat down within it. She set out her bowls and holy water and her bells. Lighting a match, she set a white piece of paper on fire and caught the embers in her hand before dropping them in the first bowl. Filling the other two bowls with holy water, Harper closed her eyes and focused on opening a channel with the spiritual world. Although it was hard, she decided to try to call Mrs. Devereux. She focused on the name and began to ask the spirit to come before her. After several long minutes a familiar voice called her name.

"Harper girl, you can stop calling me. I heard you already."

Harper opened her eyes and smiled in relief. "I'm so glad you're here!"

"I'm not," Mrs. Devereux retorted. "Of all the places I've been, this is the worst. There is something seriously wrong with this land. It feels empty."

"Yes!" Harper said. "This place is inhabited by

the Razu! Soul eaters! You have to get my grandma! I think Michael is in trouble, and I'm not going to be able to protect him myself."

The spirit stilled completely. "Rakshasa. I haven't heard of them in centuries," she whispered.

"Rakshasa?" Harper asked. "No, I said Razu."

"Razu is a perversion of what they once were," Mrs. Devereux explained impatiently. "The Rakshasa were first named in Indian mythology. They are a monstrous race of immortal creatures. The Hindus called them the Rakshasa, the Japanese called them the Rasetsu, the Indonesians called them Rakus. Most Asian cultures are aware of what they are, due to the spread of Buddhism. Not all Rakshasa were bad. But a small group of them, the ones you call Razu, were the worst of them all, demanding to be worshipped as gods and eating human flesh as sacrifice. They became so warped, so evil and dangerous, that no one could defeat them." Harper nodded but wished Mrs. Devereux would skip the history lesson. "Only one shaman was powerful enough to stop them, a woman named Baritegi. She was the only human to have ever walked into death and back to life. Because of her abilities to control both the world of the dead and the world of the living, Baritegi was able to trap the Razu in the spiritual realm to save humanity."

Mrs. Devereux shook her head. "This is bad. They are supposed to be imprisoned for eternity."

"They've been eating the souls of people with the brightest auras," Harper said.

"They must intend to try to escape. No wonder this land is a spiritual wasteland. I must leave immediately, or they will come for me."

"But my grandma . . ."

"Shh, Harper! I will tell her everything, but you are in grave danger," Mrs. Devereux said. "The reason the Razu can walk the land now is because the closer we get to All Hallows' Eve, the blurrier the line between the spiritual realm and the human world becomes. You must hide your aura! Like you did before. Hide Harper. You are in terrible danger. I will send the madam to you."

And with that, the spirit vanished.

Harper didn't know how Mrs. Devereux was going to send her grandmother, but she felt a slight relief in knowing that a message would reach her.

But what did Mrs. Devereux mean that Harper was in danger? How was she to hide her aura? Harper looked around and saw that the ghost girl had also disappeared. The hairs on the back of her neck rose up as a creepy sensation began to overwhelm her. Something was coming.

Frightened, Harper sat still and closed her eyes and then willed herself into absolute calmness. She remembered Rose telling her that her aura had been muted when she couldn't remember her past. Harper needed Rose. Rose would know what to do. But her friend was gone. All she had left were her memories. Thoughts of Rose filled her head—her laughter, her voice, her teasing. Harper missed her old friend so much. She imagined herself walking in a green meadow with soft tall grass and colorful wildflowers scattered in vibrant patches all around her. She took a deep breath. The crisp fresh air smelled of grass and flowers and mist. In the distance, she could hear someone calling her name. She recognized the voice immediately. She turned, and there was Rose. Not ghost Rose, but Rose alive and beautiful. Harper ran to hug her friend and gasped to feel a warm body and strong arms grab her and spin her around. They both laughed in delight as they lay down in the soft grass, their heads close together as they pointed out the shapes of the clouds in the bright blue sky.

"Rose, I know this is just a dream," Harper said, "but it feels so real."

"It is real," Rose said. "I'm here for you, whenever you need me."

After several more minutes of laughter and reminiscing, Rose got up and pulled Harper to her feet. "You have to go," she said. "It's safe now."

"I don't want to leave yet," Harper pleaded.

Rose smiled and gave her a tight hug. "I'm always here for you if you need me. But someone else needs you more right now."

With that, Rose gave her a shove, and Harper felt herself falling and then abruptly woke up. Harper opened her eyes. Everything seemed normal. The oppressive fear was gone. The only difference was the little ghost who sat in front of her, staring at her in awe.

"How'd you do that?" Holly asked.

"Do what?"

"Disappear!"

"I what?"

"I mean your aura disappeared," Holly said. "At first you were glowing bright silver and then it dimmed to like a faint blue and then disappeared. Even now, you're still not as bright as before."

"I don't know," Harper said. "But I had the help of a friend." A pang of sadness hit her as she missed Rose.

"A monster came," Holly said. "He was looking for that other spirit lady. I tried to stay with you, but I was so scared. And then you disappeared."

"Did you see the monster come?" Harper asked.

Holly shook her head. "I hided."

"How were you able to hide from it?"

"I tried not to be afraid, even though they feel so scary. I think of my mommy and daddy and puppies and kittens until the monsters go away," Holly said.

Harper thought that was interesting. "So, if you don't see the monsters, how do you know when they're coming?"

"I can feel them," Holly said. "It's the scariest feeling in the world. Like I'm too scared to even cry."

Harper understood that feeling completely. Her arms were covered in goose bumps. She didn't want to think about what it would be like to actually come face-to-face with a real live Razu.

"Holly, you said that all the people in the grove had marks on their necks like the one Michael has. Did you and your parents have marks, too?"

Holly cocked her head to the side as she thought. "I had one, but my parents didn't." She started to cry. "It was my fault they died."

"No, Holly, it's not your fault at all! These are

monsters," Harper said. "They are evil. They targeted you. They are at fault. And we have to stop them. Will you help me?"

Holly nodded, her little face determined.

MRS. NAKAMURA'S CHARMS AND AMULETS SHOP

Monday, October 30

Olivia had invited them to tour the island with her. Leo was not interested and stayed home, while Kelly had plans with friends she'd made.

Harper and Dayo decided that they should go back to the local market and talk to the lady with the toy boat stand where Michael had gotten his boat. The more Harper thought about the woman's reaction, the more it bothered her. She'd known that the mark meant something bad. What Harper wanted to know was, what exactly did that woman know?

Olivia had a shuttle bus take them to the center of the small town square. As the girls walked toward the market, they ran into Kelly with a group of teenage girls, all wearing similar short dresses in vibrant colors.

"You look like a flower garden," Michael said as he grinned up at them.

Kelly and the girls laughed as they all surrounded Michael to rave about how cute he was.

"Where are you going?" Harper asked. She was eager for them to be on their way.

Kelly pointed to the street opposite the outside market, where there was a mall with higher-end boutique stores. "We're going to do some shopping, and there's an old-fashioned ice cream parlor in there. Do you want to meet up later?"

"Maybe," Harper said.

"Suit yourself."

But before they could leave, Harper noticed that one of Kelly's friends, a pretty girl with long brown hair, had a triangular bruise on her neck, just like Michael's. Harper stepped closer to ask her quietly how she got the mark.

The girl rubbed it self-consciously and smiled. "I don't really know," she replied. "I was having weird nightmares, and I think I must have hit myself or something. But don't worry. It's nothing."

"What kind of nightmares?" Harper asked.

Before the girl could answer, Kelly interrupted.

"Harper, leave Megan alone. She doesn't want to talk about it. We have to go now."

The girls left with waves and smiles and laughter.

"We don't want old-time ice cream, Harper?" Michael asked, his face a little sad.

"Sure we do," Harper replied. "But maybe on our own, without all those girls pinching your cheeks, telling you how cute you are."

"Oh yeah." Michael scowled. "I hate it when they pinch my cheeks."

Dayo and Olivia laughed. They held his hands and swung him all the way across the street. Harper walked ahead, anxious to get to the stall with the wooden toy boats. The same little girl was there from before, organizing a large set of wooden boats. She waved at Michael and invited him to play with her.

The mother came out and smiled at them. "Can I help you girls?"

"Yes," Harper said. "Last time I was here, there was a boy who had a mark on his neck that seemed to scare you. Can you tell me why?"

The woman looked at her blankly. "I have no idea what you're talking about," she said.

"Let me show you," Harper said grimly. "It looked like this." She pointed at Michael's neck and watched as the woman's face paled.

"I'm sorry, but you'll have to leave," she said, grabbing her daughter by the hand and yanking her away.

"No, we won't," Harper retorted. "You have to tell us what this means."

The woman was shaking her head, when Olivia stepped forward.

"Do you know who I am?" Olivia asked. "I'm Olivia Bennington, and my mother owns this entire island. I'm asking you to please answer her question."

Harper and Dayo glanced at each other in surprise, impressed by Olivia's show of authority.

The stall owner stopped, her face visibly distraught.

"I don't know what I can tell you," she replied. "All I know is that the mark is a sign of very bad luck, and I don't want that for my daughter. So please leave now."

"But what kind of bad luck?" Harper asked. "Please, if this had been your daughter who had been marked, you would want someone to talk to you."

The woman hesitated, then nodded. "Go see Mrs. Nakamura. Her store is at the very end of the market. Her sign says 'Charms and Amulets.' She may be able to help you."

Harper didn't get very far before Olivia stopped her. "What's going on?"

Harper furrowed her eyebrows as she tried to figure out what to say, when Dayo beat her to it.

"There's something weird happening on this island, and it's dangerous," Dayo said.

"Do you know the history of this place?" Harper asked sharply.

"You mean the murders? Of course," Olivia said. "But what does that have to do with Michael and the mark?"

"It was a monster," Michael announced loudly. The girls all turned to look at him. "I know it was real. It hurt me."

"What kind of monster?" Olivia asked.

Michael trembled and shrank tight against Harper's side. "It was the scariest monster I ever seen. It was very pale and had no eyes."

Olivia looked stunned. "I've had nightmares about that same monster," she said. "And lately they've been getting worse. How can this be possible?"

"Let's go find out," Harper said. They headed to the very end of the market and found a small storefront with a crooked sign that said Charms and Amulets. They walked into a cramped little space filled from top to bottom with knickknacks of all kinds.

An old wrinkled Asian woman sat behind the counter, chewing on a toothpick.

"Are you Mrs. Nakamura?" Harper asked.

She nodded but looked only at Michael, focused on the mark on his neck. Finally, she rose slowly to her feet and began shuffling around her little shop.

"The little one needs protective amulets," Mrs. Nakamura muttered as she searched through her display box. "I have just the thing for him."

Harper stood in front of the woman, trying to catch her eye. "And just what does he need protection from?"

"From the Razu," she said, still looking through her box. "They have marked him as their sacrifice."

"What's a sacrifice?" Michael asked as he looked at all the wonderful and weird things in her displays.

Harper shook her head at Mrs. Nakamura, silently asking her not to answer Michael's question. The woman nodded.

"Hey, little one, come see all the seashells I keep in this corner," she said, leading Michael away to the other side of the shop and showing him a display box filled with shells. "Can you count me out twenty pink shells? I'll give you a prize."

"Cool!" Michael said as he plopped down on the floor with the box in front of him.

Mrs. Nakamura moved back to the counter and continued sorting through her box.

"Usually they take only one or two per year," Mrs. Nakamura muttered. "But this year something strange is going on. I've seen several marks, like that dreadful time in 2003. But this time they are all so young."

"Why are they going after young people this time?"

"Pure energy," Mrs. Nakamura said. "Only the young have auras that are clear and unpolluted by the sins of age."

"You've seen the marks every year?" Harper asked.

Mrs. Nakamura nodded, her wrinkly face sad. "When I first came to the island, forty years ago, my friend's son was marked and disappeared. My friend just thought he ran away. But it haunted me. That mark. He disappeared the night of Halloween. Ever since then, I've noticed a pattern. A person would disappear on the thirty-first and they always had the mark. And that person would always have a bright aura.

"Aha," she said as she pulled out a bunch of

old pennies with holes punched through them. She pulled out coils of copper wire and began to weave an intricate and pretty design around a penny, making each coin into a work of art. She worked quickly, and as soon as one was done, she would tie it onto a thin leather cord, making a necklace with three pennies.

"These old pennies are real copper, not like the fake-copper new ones they make nowadays," she said. She was making four necklaces. "Copper is good for masking your aura. Gold is better but much too expensive."

"You said they only took one or two a year but this year you saw many who are marked?" Olivia asked. "What can we do?"

Mrs. Nakamura gave her a look. "You cannot fight the gods," she said. "We are but mortal. All we can do is try to hide from them. That is what these amulets are for."

"But we have to warn them!" Dayo said.

The old lady sighed. "Every year I try to warn them. Only the locals know what to do. The tourists just think I'm crazy. I try to give them my amulets for free, and beg them to wear them. But they never listen."

"Why do you stay?" Dayo asked. "Why does anyone

stay if they know what happens here?"

Mrs. Nakamura stopped what she was doing and looked at them all. "I know it is hard to understand, but most of us don't have any place to go because we don't have money. The Bennington family attracted everyone here by giving them rent-free homes. And charging next to nothing to rent a space in the marketplace. They even subsidize all the town folks, to make us stay. We can't afford to live anywhere else."

Harper and Dayo looked at Olivia, who nodded. "My mom explained it was because tourists wouldn't come if the island didn't have locals."

Mrs. Nakamura snorted. "And also for when the tourists don't come."

Olivia shook her head furiously. "My mother has nothing to do with these disappearances. How dare you accuse her of that!"

"Not accusing her personally," Mrs. Nakamura said. "After all, she's only part of the company's board. And this policy was around long before she came into power."

"See?" Olivia said triumphantly.

Mrs. Nakamura finished one necklace and put it over Harper's head. "You and your little brother have strong auras," she said. "But your aura is so strong I can almost smell it."

"Smell it?" Harper thought that was odd. "What does it smell like?"

Mrs. Nakamura took a deep whiff. "You smell like sunshine and electricity."

Harper looked at Dayo and Olivia, who looked as confused as she did.

"You smell like power," Mrs. Nakamura said. She finished the necklaces and handed one each to Dayo and Olivia and then put the last one over Michael's head. He was still absorbed in sorting through his shells.

"There—this is the best I can do," Mrs. Nakamura sighed. "Keep your copper amulets on at all times while on this island. And whatever you do, stay away from Gorgon Grove, especially on Halloween!"

"Mrs. Nakamura," Harper asked, "is there anyone who got away from them?"

"Only know of one," she replied. "Her father." Mrs. Nakamura pointed at Olivia.

They all looked to stare at Olivia's ashen face. "My father who deserted me?"

"He didn't mean to desert you, my dear," Mrs. Nakamura said. "I know, because he came to me seeking amulets for you and your mother. I made one for each of you, even though you weren't even born yet."

Olivia's eyes began to tear up. "You mean he did care for me?"

"Oh yes, he loved you dearly, but he was so afraid for you," she said. "He told me that this was a curse on the Bennington family because of his grandfather, who made a pact with the gods. He told me that he believed that if he left, then the curse would leave the island with him. But as long as a Bennington was on the island, it would be doomed."

"But if that's true, why are the monsters still here?" Harper asked.

"Because she is a Bennington," Mrs. Nakamura said. "So, the curse remains."

"You mean if Olivia leaves, the island will not be cursed?" Dayo asked.

Mrs. Nakamura shook her head. "Nothing is that simple," she replied. "Mr. Bennington knew he could be killed for leaving the island. But it was a risk he was willing to take for his family's sake."

"Did he make it?" Olivia asked. "Is he still alive?"

"I don't know," Mrs. Nakamura said. "I never heard from him again."

The girls left the little shop feeling overwhelmed with everything they'd learned. Only Michael seemed happy and unconcerned. Mrs. Nakamura had given him a small bag filled with beautiful seashells, and he was so proud of all that he'd collected. Before they'd left, Harper had remembered Kelly and her friend Megan. She asked Mrs. Nakamura for two more necklaces.

As they headed back to the shuttle, Olivia was very quiet.

"Olivia, are you okay?" Dayo asked.

She nodded. "I'm just glad to know that my dad really did care about me and that he didn't abandon me for no reason. But what can we do about these gods?"

"They're not gods, they're monsters," Harper said. "And the most important thing we can do is to keep away from Gorgon Grove."

"But what about all the people already marked?" Dayo asked. "We have to save them."

Harper rubbed her eyes. She just wanted to protect her brother. "What are we supposed to do?"

"Maybe we can set guards around the grove and stop anyone from going there," Dayo said.

"Good idea!" Olivia said excitedly. "I'll ask my mom to do that right away!"

"But make sure the guards aren't too close to the grove, either," Harper cautioned. "Otherwise they might get . . ."

"Right, so I'll ask my mom to have guards stationed on all the ways into and around Gorgon Grove," she said. "Maybe even cordon it off with that police-tape stuff."

"That's a great idea!" Harper said with a rush of relief. It felt good to know they had a plan to save the others.

"There's a big party Halloween evening," Olivia said. "We should all go together."

"Yes, and stick together and watch out for each other."

The girls shook hands. "Deal."

Michael piped up. "Oh boy, a Halloween party! Can I go as Iron Man?"

The girls broke out in relieved laughter for the first time all day.

SURPRISE GUEST

Tuesday, October 31—Afternoon

The doorbell rang, and Leo went to answer it. He came back into the living room, where they were all sitting, with a puzzled look on his face.

"Harper, there's someone at the door for you," he said. "He says he has a package for you from your grandma."

This was so odd that she hesitated. Kelly was upstairs getting ready for the party, while her parents had taken Michael to his last camp day. Uncle Justin and Aunt Caroline were both at the hotel working. Why would her grandmother send a package through a strange man?

Dayo got up and went with her to the door. They

opened it to find a tall thin man with a gaunt face. Something about him was very familiar to Harper, as if she knew who he was but couldn't remember. Behind him, she could see the small hotel shuttle bus, as the driver patiently waited in the driveway.

"Are you Harper?" he asked.

Harper nodded, and he handed her a large package. Harper recognized the writing immediately. It was from her grandma Lee.

"How did you get this?" she asked suspiciously.

The man gave a sad smile. "It's a long story, but the answer is in the letter your grandmother included. Go ahead and read it. I'll wait out here until you're done."

She closed and locked the door and then went upstairs with Dayo to open the package in private. Inside she found the heavy bells that Grandma Lee had used during the soul-eater exorcism. There was a long letter inside it also.

Dear Harper,

For the first time in my life I am frightened, because I am so far away and there's nothing I can do to help you. I am desperate to come to you, but I had a bit of a fall and have broken my hip. Doctor says I'm not able to move for a while. But don't

*worry about me, I'm okay. It's all of you that I'm
worried about.*

*Mrs. Devereux is suspicious about my fall.
It happened just as I was getting ready to go to
you. Something there doesn't want me to come.
So, I'm sending you all I can to help protect you
and Michael and anyone else who needs it. That
includes the person who is bringing you the package.
The bells are very powerful, but only use them if
attacked. Mrs. Devereux has discovered that the
Razu are trying to escape from their island prison.
They need thirteen more souls this Halloween
evening, to unlock the realms and free themselves.
They will choose those souls with the strongest auras
in order to make sure the spell will work. That is
why you and Michael are in so much danger. If you
can hide from them and stay away from the grove,
they may not be able to break through. However,
if they come for you, then you must use the bells.
Remember what we did to the small soul eater. That
is the power of these bells.*

*Whatever you do, you must NOT be anywhere
near Gorgon Grove during the darkest part of
Halloween night. That is when they will begin their
spell of release and when their power will be greatest.*

Fighting one Razu is hard enough—all four will be impossible.

You must be wondering who this person is that I entrusted such an important package to. His name is Todd Bennington, and it was his grandfather who started this mess. He has been hiding from the Razu these fourteen years, but Mrs. Devereux found him and made him come to me. He can help you. He may be the key to stopping the curse.

Be safe, my darling grandchildren. I will pray for you.

Love,

Grandma

Dayo and Harper looked at each other in stunned amazement. "That's Olivia's father!"

Immediately, they rushed down and took him around the back to sit on the outside patio.

"This used to be my house," he said with a slight smile. "Looks so different now."

"Olivia and her mom live on the other side of the resort," Harper said. "Where the secret cove is."

Todd grew very still. "That's close to the grove," he whispered. "They're in danger."

"We're all in danger, sir," Harper snapped. "My

grandmother tells me you can help us. Please tell us how."

He nodded distractedly.

"When I first inherited the hotel, I had no idea about the Razu," he said. "I was just a kid. Nobody told me about the curse and the terrible deal my grandfather had agreed to. I didn't realize it myself until I was visited by one of those monsters."

His shaking fingers reached into a pocket to pull out a pack of cigarettes.

Dayo quickly grabbed them away. "No smoking," she said. "We're kids. Still growing."

Todd nodded. "Sorry about that." He ran a shaky hand through his dirty-blond hair. "What I didn't know is that my ancestors have been hiding the evidence of the Razu's hunger for nearly a century. Once the Razu chose a victim, it was my grandfather, and then my father, who would dispose of the body in the ocean."

Harper gasped. Her vision of the bodies in the water when she'd gone snorkeling was true, then. All the bodies must still be somewhere deep in the water.

"That's really bad and wrong!" Harper was shocked. "It's accesso . . . accesso . . ."

"Accessory to murder," Dayo said. "But actually,

they're accomplices. They helped the murders happen."

"That makes them just as bad as the monsters! Even worse! Why would they do that?"

"Because they couldn't afford an investigation that would stop tourists from coming," Todd said. "The police on the island are all bought and paid for by the Bennington family, but still. Annual dead bodies would be a tourism killer."

"But to hide them so no one would ever know what happened to them . . . ," Dayo said. She looked really upset. "Your grandfather was evil."

"Yes, I agree," Todd said mildly. "My grandfather and my father were both bad. I couldn't do it. I refused. For years, I just wouldn't help the Razu. And that's why they murdered all those people."

Harper felt bad for him, he looked so guilty.

He closed his eyes. "Sixteen people dead. Their bodies ripped apart and shown all over the news. And that little girl. Every night I can still see their faces."

He rubbed his head as if he was in pain. "After that terrible night, they told me if I didn't help them they would kill me. They even marked me." He pointed to his neck, where a triangular scar could be seen. His was different from Michael's and the others. It wasn't just a bruise; it was clear that it was a scar from a wound. "It's why I left. I thought if I was gone, then they wouldn't have anyone else to help them. I thought the curse would end with me. But I was wrong."

"I don't get it," Harper said. "Why do they need you? You get rid of bodies, but that's more for you than for them. What do they need you for?"

"They need people who can see auras, because they have no eyes," Todd said. "They hunt by fear. They can smell it. And they are so frightening to look at, it was easy for them to hunt. But because they're stuck in the spiritual plane, they can only send out their spiritual projections. Very few people can actually see them. It's a curse of the Benningtons that we have the ability. So, we tell them where their victims will be, and they send their projection out to mark them. Only at Gorgon Grove can they physically manifest."

"That's so wrong," Dayo whispered.

"But who are the Razu working with now?" Harper asked.

"I don't know. It has to be a family member, but the only one left of my bloodline is my daughter," he said.

"It's your wife," Harper said with absolute certainty. She thought about the coldness she'd felt when she'd met Olivia's mom for the first time.

Todd was shaking his head. "No way, my wife would never do anything like this. Besides, she doesn't have the ability."

"You don't know that for sure," Harper said. "She might be like me."

"Or she got it during her pregnancy. If she had a Bennington baby, and the baby had the ability, it's possible she got it also," Dayo said.

"Yes, and you said it yourself," Harper said. "There's no one else."

They were all silent as Todd dropped his head into his hands in a pose of despair.

"Oh no," Dayo said, sitting straight up with a concerned look on her face. "Harper, if it's Olivia's mom, then Olivia asking for guards around the grove is useless."

"I should go see her," Todd said.

"No!" Harper shouted. "She's already going to be so suspicious about us talking to Olivia. You can't go to her right now."

"But what am I supposed to do?"

"Well, why did you come here, anyway?" Harper asked. "I mean, I'm glad you brought me my grandmother's bells, but why did you come back? Aren't you in danger?"

Todd looked up. His eyes were filled with tears. "I've been running all these years, thinking I was keeping the danger from my family. Turns out I led it right to them." He let out a shaky breath. "I have to make things right. I have to fix this and break the curse."

"But how?" Dayo asked.

"I'll offer myself as sacrifice," he said.

"I'm sorry," Dayo said, ever practical, "but how does that break the curse?"

He looked stunned. "I just assumed that it would—sacrificing myself for my loved ones."

"No offense, sir, but that's not gonna work," Dayo said.

"Yeah, they're just going to take you and everyone else also," Harper said. She sat staring at her grandmother's bells. "But if we all work together, maybe we can destroy them."

"I'll do anything," Todd said.

"The bells. What they do is call all the souls that have been eaten by the Razu and pull them out to the light." Harper was thinking aloud. "The Razu aren't the only ones more powerful at the darkest part of the night. So are the spirits. And they will be longing to be free. We need to help move them to freedom."

"I don't understand," Todd said.

"My grandmother and I encountered a smaller Razu, a soul eater. We were able to defeat it by releasing all the souls within it all at once," Harper said. "We need to do that to all four of the Razu. If they've been doing this for centuries, then the souls they've eaten must number in the thousands. If I call down the spiritual bridge close enough, their yearning for the light might break them free."

"They'd explode out of the monster," Dayo said.

Harper nodded.

"Can you really do that?" Todd asked.

"I'm gonna try," she said. "But we need help. Can you get Mrs. Nakamura?"

Todd jumped to his feet. "I know where she lives."

"Tell her I need a lot of holy water, gallons of it! As many large plates or bowls as she can get and all her copper wire," Harper said.

"When and where do we meet?"

"Grandma said they will be active at the darkest part of the night," Harper said. "I think she means midnight."

Dayo nodded. "Yeah, the darkest part of the night is the halfway point between sunset and sunrise." She pulled out her phone to search the times. "Sunrise is at seven a.m. and sunset is at seven twenty p.m. So, the darkest will be around one a.m."

"Then let's meet at ten at the grove," Harper said. "I want enough time to set up and then get away before they arrive. And, Mr. Bennington, please don't forget to ask Mrs. Nakamura for a copper amulet."

Todd pulled a necklace out from under his shirt, showing the copper wire-wrapped pennies on his necklace. "I've never taken it off."

"Ask her to make more," Harper said. "A lot more. We're going to need them for anyone who is marked."

"Harper, your grandma said we can't be there," Dayo said.

"Don't worry, we'll be long gone before midnight."

Dayo looked worried. "But what happens if we don't get out in time?"

Harper had no good answer for her friend.

HALLOWEEN

Tuesday, October 31—Night

Harper, Dayo, Leo, and Michael stood at the entrance of the Royal Ballroom, gawking at all the people dressed in wild costumes at the party. They watched as Kelly, wearing a fancy flapper outfit, raced off to meet her friends. Harper had to admit that her sister and her friends looked great in their matching dresses, with all their sequined fringe shimmying as they moved. She was staring at Megan, the girl with the mark.

"Do you think Kelly will give Megan the necklace?" Dayo asked.

"Yeah," Harper said. "But I don't think Megan will wear it. Kelly refused to wear hers because it doesn't go with her outfit."

"You're right," Dayo sighed. "Maybe it will be enough if she keeps it in her purse?"

Harper looked skeptical. "I don't think it's enough." She scratched her neck where she'd started to sweat. She was not excited about her costume, which her mother had forced her to wear.

Olivia had sent over costumes for them yesterday, as they didn't have any. Michael was decked out as his favorite character, Iron Man. Dayo wore a pretty Red Riding Hood cloak over an all-black ninja outfit and mask, and called herself Red Riding Ninjahood. Dayo had refused to wear the little dress that had come with the cape, and Harper couldn't blame her. It had been way too short. Leo had on a chef's jacket and hat, which had made his father proud. But Harper was wearing a big one-piece panda suit. The hood was the panda face, and the black-and-white onesie had long sleeves and detachable footies. Harper had declined to wear the footies and had on her sneakers instead. She was unhappy because the suit was hot and she was already starting to sweat. But it was either the panda or a sexy pirate. It was no contest.

Fortunately, the ballroom was well air-conditioned.

"Come on, let's go eat!" Leo said. Before they

could head to the buffet table, Yuna caught Michael by the hand.

"Michael, you come with Mommy and Daddy," Yuna said. "There's a magic show that you will love in the other party room."

"Oh boy, a magic show!" Michael immediately pivoted to head out with Yuna.

Harper turned to follow, but her father waved her away. "Sweetheart, go with your friends," he said. "This is a little-kid show. You'll be bored."

He smiled and winked and then followed after Yuna and Michael.

Michael waved good-bye and then disappeared from view. For a moment, Harper panicked, worried that she wouldn't see him again.

"It's okay, Harper," Dayo said. "He's safe with your mom and dad."

"You're right," she sighed. "Let's go look for Olivia!"

They went searching for Olivia but were perturbed to find her missing. Calls to her cell phone were going directly to voice mail. It was unlike Olivia to not meet them.

Finally, they found someone who told them that Olivia was home sick.

"This is really weird," Harper said.

"Her mom must be sick, too," Leo said. "I heard my mom saying it was unlike Mrs. Bennington to miss tonight's big bash, because so many important people are here."

Harper and Dayo traded worried looks.

"Do you think she's in trouble?" Dayo asked. "Should we try to go over to her house?"

Leo stared at both of them. "What in the world are you talking about?"

The girls ignored him. "We haven't told her about the new plans," Dayo said.

"We can't," Harper said. "It's still her mother."

"We're not sure," Dayo said, but bit her lip when Harper gave her a disbelieving look. "Yeah, it has to be her."

"Who has to be what?" Leo asked.

"You should tell him," Dayo said.

"Tell me what?" Leo demanded. "Wait, is it about the ghosts?"

Both Dayo and Harper nodded.

"I don't want to know! Don't tell me! I'm gonna go eat dinner by myself," Leo said and stormed off.

Harper smirked. "Should we eat dinner now?"

"I'm not even hungry. I'm too scared to eat," Dayo said.

"Me too." Harper looked at her watch. It was six

thirty. They still had a few hours to go. "But we have to eat something now. We have almost three hours to kill."

"Don't say kill!"

"Sorry."

The girls headed toward the buffet table, where they were once again awed by the amount and variety of food spread out in front of white-gloved servers.

"I don't even know where to start," Dayo sighed.

Harper grabbed a plate and got on line. "Not me—I know exactly what I want."

She held her plate up to be served roast beef with potatoes and salad. "I only got the salad to make you happy," she said to Dayo.

Dayo smiled and got the same thing. After filling their plates with more goodies, they were looking for a place to sit when Dayo spied Leo at a back table by himself. She nudged Harper and forced her toward the table. They sat with Leo as waiters served them ice water.

"Leo, don't you want to know what's been happening on this island?" Dayo asked.

He shook his head vigorously. "I don't see that little ghost girl anymore, and I'd like to keep it that way."

Harper snorted. "Chicken."

Leo glared at her. "Not wanting to see ghosts isn't being a chicken, it's being smart," he retorted.

"That little girl died in the Gorgon Grove massacre," Harper said. "Her whole family died that night."

They were all quiet for a moment.

"I'm sorry about that," Leo said. "But still. I don't want to hear about it."

"She was marked on the neck by the monsters who were after her," Harper continued relentlessly. "The same mark that's now on Michael's neck."

Leo's head whipped around to stare at her. "Is he in danger?"

"We're all in danger," Dayo said.

With a heavy sigh, Leo put his fork down. "Tell me everything."

Harper and Dayo explained all that they'd encountered and discovered. When they were done, Leo looked even more pale and frightened than he had the first time they'd seen him.

"And what the heck do you want *me* to do?" he asked.

"Just help us keep an eye on Michael," Harper said. "Keep him safe no matter what. We'll end up leaving here around nine to take Michael home. The adults are all going back to the party, and Dayo and I have to go meet Mr. Bennington. So, that means we need you to watch Michael."

Leo nodded. "I promise."

They ate the rest of their meal in silence. When they were done, Harper got up and stretched and pointed to the dessert table.

"We need a lot of sugar to get us through the night," she announced.

Dayo enthusiastically agreed.

By eight o'clock, the trio were too nervous and agitated to stay at the party anymore. They went to the little-kid party room, where Michael was waiting for his balloon octopus. They were able to convince Harper's parents to take them all home early. As predicted, Yuna and Peter returned to the party after kissing Michael good night.

With Michael in bed, Harper asked Leo to find all the pennies in the house.

"How do you know which pennies are full copper?" Dayo asked.

"I'm just gonna pull any penny older than 1970," Harper replied. Using scraps of fabric and twine, Harper made small pouches filled with the old pennies.

The three of them worked quietly and steadily. The only noise was the jingling of the coins and the ticking of a nearby clock.

Harper paused. In the distance, she heard a faint drumming.

"Dayo, do you hear drums?"

Her friend sat up and cupped her ear. "I don't hear anything."

The drumming was getting louder.

"It's so loud now," Harper said.

Dayo's eyes widened. "What is it? Why can't I hear it?"

Leo looked at Harper in total confusion.

Dayo reached over and grabbed Harper's hands and gasped loudly. "I hear it now, too!"

"It wants me to follow it," Harper said dreamily.

"Don't even think about it, Harper Raine!"

"I already am," Harper said. She frowned. "Where am I?"

"Harper, what's happening?" Dayo shook Harper's hand, but Harper didn't feel it. She was deep into a new vision.

She was walking through a hot, humid jungle. The beating of the drums had stopped, and all she heard was an eerie silence of a jungle devoid of life. And then she heard a soft chanting. Following the low murmuring voice, she came into a clearing and recoiled in terror. Harper badly wanted to run away, but something kept her glued to the spot. She'd come across what looked like a small seaside village empty of any people. Blood and body parts were strewn all over the place, leading to a grove of large twisty trees with the blue ocean behind it. A dark-haired, brown-skinned woman holding a staff stood between the village and the trees. Chanting. But what was horrifying was not the dead villagers but the gigantic creatures lying on the ground, entangled all together under the shadow of the trees. They were soul eaters that were almost as big as elephants. Harper counted four of them. She didn't know if they were sleeping or under a spell, but they lay unmoving in front of the chanting woman.

A loud snore cut through the silence. The Razu were sleeping. Blood covered their faces and clawlike hands. The pale tree trunks were splattered in red gore and the bloody bones and skulls of numerous humans littered the ground around them.

Harper's attention was drawn back to the fearless woman. This must be the shaman Baritegi. Her long black hair was plaited into a thick braid. Her simple robes of red and yellow were striking against her dark skin. She spoke in a lilting, musical language that Harper didn't understand but vaguely recognized.

The shaman raised her bare arms and shook her staff at the sky. Muttering, she moved her arms in a rhythmic circle as the Razu remained motionless. Over and over she swirled her arms, as the sky turned a dark angry gray while lightning and thunder cracked above them. It began to rain hard. Harper had to wipe her face in order to see. She caught a movement from one of the Razu. They were beginning to wake up. Harper wanted to warn the shaman. But the thunder drowned out her voice.

The Razu closest to the shaman raised its head and sniffed at the air. It snarled as the others began to stir also.

Harper gasped as the first Razu hurled itself toward the shaman. And then, with a sharp crack of the staff to the ground, the shaman pointed to the sky and channeled a bolt of lightning from the air into her hands. It was so bright Harper had to shield herself from the light. The Razu stopped in confusion. Something was happening. With a great heave, the shaman threw the lightning bolt into the center of the largest tree, where it formed a whirling opening, like a tornado. It swallowed the Raku into the whirlwind one by one and then sealed itself completely shut, leaving only a grossly deformed tree trunk behind, pulsing with light.

The shaman still held the lightning bolt that was coursing through her staff. She directed it at her feet and swiftly sent it pulsing through the ground. Harper could feel the earth rumbling, and a crack formed between the shaman and the Razu tree. The land shifted and separated. And an island formed as the masses broke apart. Only then did Harper realize she was on the wrong side. She was on Razu Island, watching the shaman walking away. Panic filled her, and she tried to run toward the water to swim back to the mainland. But she was still frozen, rooted to the spot. She looked down and saw two large claws grasping her shoes.

Harper screamed.

Dayo screamed and Leo jumped.

"You scared me!" Dayo sputtered. "Are you okay? Was it another vision?"

Harper nodded. "The tree," she said. "They're in the tree."

"What? But how?"

Before Harper could explain, Holly suddenly appeared.

"I heard the drums, and Michael got up and just started walking out!" she cried.

Harper leaped to her feet and raced up the stairs,

Dayo and Leo close behind her. Michael's room was empty. She hurried into her room, grabbed her shaman bag and ran downstairs.

Holly was floating next to her as they ran. "Which way did he go?" Harper asked grimly.

"Follow me." Holly flew in front of them.

Harper followed as fast as she could and was so relieved when she spotted Michael's form up ahead.

"There he is!" she shouted.

They all raced toward him, when a heavy mist appeared rapidly, and they could no longer see anything. Harper froze and fell to the ground as Dayo and Leo crashed into her.

"We can't see anything," Leo said. "What do we do?"

"Look, there's no fog at our feet," Dayo said.

She was right. The mist seemed to hover several inches off the ground.

Dayo took out her phone and used the flashlight app. It penetrated the fog a little, giving them barely a one-foot radius that they could see.

"Holly!" Harper shouted.

The little ghost appeared immediately.

"What happened? Why aren't you following me?" Holly asked.

"We can't see through this fog," Harper said.

Holly looked confused. "What fog?"

"There's a heavy fog surrounding us right now," Harper explained. "We can't see where to go because of it. If you can't see it, then it mustn't be real."

"So, what do we do? He's getting away," Holly said.

"Holly, if you can't see the fog, then you can still lead the way, but you have to stay real close to us so we can see you," Dayo said.

She reached over to hold Harper's and Leo's hands. "We need to stick close together or we'll get lost."

They followed Holly closely, but with the thickness of the fog, it was really slow going.

"This is no good!" Harper cried. "We're losing him."

She opened her bag and pulled out her *mudang* bells. Shaking them hard, she yelled, "Go away, fog!"

Before her, a clear pathway opened up as the fog reacted to her bells.

"How'd you do that?" Leo asked.

"This isn't real fog," Harper said. "It's created by the Razu."

She shook the bells hard in front of her, and cleared an almost ten-foot radius around them. Now they could follow Holly, who flew ahead. Soon, they saw Michael's little form trudging forward.

"Michael!" Harper shouted. "Michael, Michael, Michael!"

Both Leo and Dayo started shouting his name also. Michael stopped and turned toward them in surprise. He smiled up at Holly, who fluttered about him.

As they reached his side, they heard him say, "Holly, watcha doing out here?"

"Michael, you have to go home!" Harper yelled.

"Sorry, Harper. I was following the drums." He turned as if he was listening to something else, and he began to walk away again. Harper grabbed him and picked him up, walking quickly in the other direction. "No, you need to go home right now."

"But the drums," Michael said in a dreamy voice. "I need to go find them."

"No, you don't. Come on, everyone, let's talk to Michael really loudly so he can't hear those nasty drums anymore."

Leo started singing a terrible tune in a terrible voice while Dayo recited a long and boring poem and Harper repeated *Green Eggs and Ham* in its entirety. In this manner, they returned back to the house. Once safely inside, Harper put headphones on Michael's ears and told him to stay in bed and not take them off for any reason.

"Leo, you stay here and make sure Michael doesn't leave this room!"

"Don't worry, he'll be safe with me," he said.

"Harper, it's nine forty-five," Dayo said. "How will we get to the grove on time?"

"There's a golf cart in the back of the house," Leo said. "It's just like driving the race cars at the track."

Harper grinned evilly. "Where's the key?"

KELLY TO THE RESCUE

Tuesday, October 31—Later that night

Dayo sat nervously next to Harper. "You sure you know how to drive this thing?"

"Yep," Harper said. "I had to listen to Kelly complaining about driver's ed for months. Also, I've played lots of *Super Mario Kart*."

"That doesn't reassure me!"

"We'll be fine!"

"Do you even know where you're going?"

"That's what GPS is for."

Harper turned on her phone's GPS, started the electric engine, and maneuvered onto the road. After a few jerky stops and starts, she drove the cart smoothly.

"This road isn't on GPS, Harper," Dayo announced.

"Rats!"

"I'll show you the way," Holly piped up as she suddenly appeared before them. She was floating in the space between the steering wheel and the dashboard.

Harper braked suddenly with a loud *Gah!* "That would be great!" she said. "But please do me a big favor and never scare me like that again."

Like before, they followed the little ghost over the winding roads. They passed the resort and found themselves driving right by Olivia's house. It was pitch-black.

"Do you think they're all sleeping?" Dayo asked.

"I've got a bad feeling," Harper said.

Just then, it began to rain hard. They continued to drive quickly down the roads, following Holly through what became pouring rain. Even though the cart had a roof, they were soon soaked as the winds drove the rain sideways and bounced off the ground into their faces. Lightning and thunder filled the skies, and suddenly a tree came crashing down in front of the cart.

All three of them screamed.

"Why did you scream, Holly?" Harper asked after they all caught their breaths. "The tree can't hurt you."

"I screamed because you both did," Holly said. "It was fun."

Dayo started laughing. "All this fun is gonna give me nightmares for life."

Harper had gotten out of the cart and was looking for a way around the tree. She returned to them, shaking her head. "No way around—we're gonna have to climb over it."

They left the golf cart and were about to climb over the tree when they heard the beeping of another golf cart. Surprised, they turned to find Kelly driving toward them with an angry expression on her dripping-wet face.

Both Harper and Dayo froze in shock, their mouths gaping open. Kelly was still wearing her flapper costume, but now she looked like a glittery drowned cat.

"What's gotten into you guys? Mom and Dad are going to kill you, Harper! Come home right now!"

"I thought you were still at the party. How'd you find us?" Harper asked.

"I broke one of my heels, so I went back to the house to get a new pair, and when I didn't see you guys, I made Leo tell me where you went! And I'm so annoyed because it was really hard tracking you with

Find My iPhone because you weren't on any main roads!"

Harper shared an impressed look with Dayo. "She tracked us."

"I can't believe I'm missing the rest of the party because of you guys," Kelly ranted. "Just look at me! I'm a mess! Now get in that cart and come back right now!"

Harper shook her head. "People are in danger. We have to save them."

"I don't want to play games with you, Harper. I just want to get dry! Now let's go!" Kelly reached out and grabbed Harper by the arm and pulled hard.

At that moment, Holly surged into Kelly's face. "You leave Harper alone!"

Kelly screamed and fell back with a splash into a mud puddle. "Did you see that? Did you see a little girl?"

"That's Holly," Dayo said as she pulled Kelly up. "We have to go. You can either come with us or go home."

Harper nodded. "I'm sorry, Kelly. We have to go save your friend Megan."

"Megan?" Kelly asked in complete surprise. "What does this have to do with her?"

"She's probably been taken by the monsters," Dayo explained as Harper climbed over the tree. "It's why we asked you to give her the penny necklace—for protection—but I'm guessing she didn't wear it, and neither did you."

"No," Kelly replied slowly as she followed Dayo over the tree. "She said it was sweet but it didn't match her dress. She asked me to hold it for her. And then she disappeared. I figured she went back to her room."

"We know where she went," Harper called back grimly. "We have to save her."

Kelly stopped. "No, Harper. We have to go home. I'm not listening to another word of this."

Before she could turn back, Harper grabbed her hand and called for Holly. The ghost girl immediately appeared in front of Kelly's face, causing her to scream.

"I'm sorry I scared you," Holly said. "But you gotta let Harper and Dayo go, or a lot of people are going to die."

Kelly followed them without another word. The rain came down harder. Harper's shoes were filled with water and caked in mud, making them hard to walk in.

"I think we're almost there!" Harper shouted.

Holly nodded and flew ahead. Harper, Dayo, and Kelly locked arms to keep going, their heads down against wind and rain, when abruptly, everything stopped. They were in the grove, shivering from the cold and wet, but relieved to be out of the rain.

Kelly blinked her eyes in bewilderment and slowly rotated in one spot. All around them the storm raged, but here, close to the trees, it was a perfect clear night.

"This is all a bad nightmare," Kelly whispered. "When I wake up in the morning, everything will be fine. I just have to get through this night."

"Harper, look!" Holly was flickering in distress.

On the ground in front of the lightning-struck tree were numerous bodies lying in a circle, their feet pointing toward the tree.

"There are twelve people here," Dayo said. "They look like they're sleeping."

"They're under a spell," Harper replied. She opened her bag and pulled out her penny pouches and placed one on each person.

"Oh no, that's Megan!" Kelly cried.

"Quick, we have to move them away from the tree," Harper said. "This is the tree that the Razu are imprisoned in. I saw it in my vision."

Dayo shuddered as she grabbed a sleeping victim

215

under the arms and dragged him away. Kelly was pulling Megan away from the tree but slipped and fell. Harper ran over to help her and noticed her bare feet covered in mud.

"What happened to your shoes?"

"When I ran out of the house, I just grabbed a pair of flip-flops. I don't even know whose they were," Kelly said. "I lost them in that crazy storm back there." She looked frightened. "This is Gorgon Grove, where those horrible murders occurred. Is Megan going to be all right?"

"That's why we're here," Harper said. "I'm hoping they can't proceed since they're missing the thirteenth sacrifice."

"But that's okay, since one of you will easily fit the bill," a voice rang out from behind them.

They turned, to see Olivia's mother pointing a gun at them. She was wearing a raincoat and boots and an angry expression.

"Mrs. Bennington," Harper said. "How could you do something so evil?"

They stared as Mrs. Bennington's face seemed to lose focus for a moment. "I'm not evil," she whispered. "You don't understand. A mother would do anything to protect her child."

"But this is wrong! You can't do this!"

"I have no choice," Mrs. Bennington whispered. "They promised not to harm Olivia. They even promised never to show themselves to her. I don't want my baby to ever know the ugly truth. That her bloodline is evil."

"You're killing innocent people!"

"If it means my child is safe, then yes. A thousand times, yes!" Mrs. Bennington shouted.

"No, Clarissa, this is not your fault." Todd Bennington finally arrived, carrying a box of things, with Mrs. Nakamura trailing behind him. They both were soaking wet.

"You!" Clarissa turned the gun on her husband. "How dare you show your face here after deserting me and your only baby!"

"I'm so sorry, love," Todd said, tears rolling down his face. He put the box down on the ground and approached his wife. "I thought I was saving you both. Instead, I cursed you."

"Do you know how hard it was?" Clarissa asked. "Do you know how your board of directors treated me? Like dirt! Like a gold digger! They thought I was stupid. Not good enough for the Bennington name. What a joke! If they only knew the truth! So, I went back to school. Got a business degree from the University of Miami. I took that boat every day to go to classes. And I taught myself everything I needed to know to make this business work. Because I had no choice! The Razu threatened to kill Olivia, just like they killed our little baby boy."

"I'm sorry . . ."

"No, you're not sorry!" she said fiercely. "You ran away. You were relieved. You were able to escape from hell on earth. And you left me and Olivia behind to save your own skin."

"You're right," he said. "I've been in hiding this whole time. I've been so afraid. Too afraid to come back and protect my family. I was wrong. So wrong. But I'm here now. Let me help you."

"You're too late," Clarissa said. "And I will never forgive you."

As the Benningtons argued, Harper and Dayo stealthily met up with Mrs. Nakamura, while Kelly continued to drag the sleeping victims as far away from the Razu tree as possible. Mrs. Nakamura brought over the box Todd had been carrying and quickly opened it. She handed them the necklaces, which they put around the necks of all the sleeping victims, then Mrs. Nakamura took out the copper wire and began to wind it around the Razu tree itself. Inside the box there were many large plastic bowls, several containers of salt, and two gallons of holy water.

"Because they all can too," Harper said, gesturing to the Benningtons and Mrs. Nakamura.

The Razu was sniffing the air, its slit-like nostrils opening and closing as it snarled and drooled. The monster tried to step out of the tree, and its flesh brushed against the copper wire, causing it to shriek in pain. It climbed up into the branches and leaped down to the ground. Two more Razu climbed out after it and came racing toward Harper, who stood in front of the others. They stopped at the salt line and murmured to each other as they circled around the salt.

"Close your eyes, and don't let them sense your fear," Harper said. "They can't find you if you aren't afraid. I know it might seem impossible not to be afraid, but any other emotion is probably fine. Be angry, be sad. Just don't be afraid."

The Razu standing before Harper made it almost impossible for her to follow through on her own words. It was more than twice the size of the soul eater she'd faced with her grandmother, with a bulk like that of a gorilla. Its huge head loomed over Harper, sharp fangs dripping with saliva and its two slit-like nostrils opening and closing as it sniffed out the fear.

Harper could hear Kelly's terror in her muffled shrieks. Her grandmother was right—Kelly definitely

221

had some spiritual sensitivity if she could see Holly from earlier and the Razu.

"Guys, I will need you to repeat the chant I'm going to do. Be as loud as you can."

The other Razu now all gathered in front of Harper. Harper filled herself with rage on behalf of Holly and her family, on behalf of all the innocent people who had been killed over the years, and for Rose. She felt the surge of fury, and she began to ring her bells and chant the binding prayer, invoking the wills of the Ancient One and the Worthy One.

"Through the power of the Ancient One, I bind you. You will do no harm. Through the power of the Worthy One, I bind you. You will do no harm. Through the power of the Ancient One, I bind you. You will do no harm. Through the power of the Worthy One, I bind you. You will do no harm."

Over and over, Harper repeated the chant, her voice raised louder by those of Dayo, Mrs. Nakamura, and the Benningtons.

"Through the power of the Ancient One, I bind you. You will do no harm. Through the power of the Worthy One, I bind you. You will do no harm."

The Razu seemed stunned by the spell as they stood unmoving in front of them. Harper could see within the distended bellies of the monsters the bright light of spiritual energy. Souls trapped for centuries, yearning to be free.

Harper placed both Wisdom and Truth in her left hand, continuing to ring them vigorously as she leaned over to pick up the Bringer, the Blessed One. The one that would bring the light to the spirits.

"Keep chanting the same chant—don't stop!" Harper yelled at the others.

And then she began to ring the Bringer. The loud melodic tolling of the bell was brighter than any of the other bells.

"May the path of light shine free and guide you! May the path of light shine free and guide you!" As she yelled into the heavens, a white light began to form over the tree. The Razu let out ear-piercing screams as the spirits inside of them began to pulsate feverishly.

As the light grew strong and bright, Harper switched chants again, this time speaking directly to all the souls.

"Come forth, dear ones! Come to the light and be free!" Harper yelled. "Come to the light and be free!"

Harper shouted and rang her bells over and over again. The moonlit path from the heavens shone even brighter. The Razu's stomachs began to pulse with light, and they shook uncontrollably until their bellies ruptured as the spirits burst through their imprisonment and headed straight for the moonlit path.

Harper grabbed hold of the Unmaker and rang it hard three times, shouting, "Be gone!"

The Razu exploded into nothingness.

Harper collapsed onto the ground, exhausted.

"Are they gone?" Dayo asked. She opened her eyes and smiled tearfully at the dancing spirits above her. "Oh, how beautiful."

Mrs. Nakamura stood with her hands clasped, crying as she gazed at the ecstatic dance of the free spirits.

Only the Benningtons stood sadly, holding up Olivia, who had not woken from her trance.

"Why isn't she snapping out of it?" Todd asked.

"Megan isn't waking up," Kelly cried out. "What's going on?"

A sudden worrying sensation filled Harper.

"Watch out, Harper! There's still one more, and she's the queen." Holly appeared before them.

"Holly!" Harper yelled. "Go to the light!"

"She's coming!" Holly screamed, then disappeared.

Olivia suddenly lurched out of her parents' arms and toward the tree. Her parents ran after her and caught her just as a hideous sound filled their ears.

Harper's head snapped up, and she grabbed her bells. "Get back in the circle!"

The Benningtons dragged Olivia into the circle and sat down, embracing her.

"Harper, help!" Kelly shouted.

Kelly was desperately holding on to Megan and a few others who had gotten up and were stepping out of the protective circle. Dayo and Mrs. Nakamura raced over while Harper made an even bigger salt circle. She rang her bell in the victims' faces and shouted at them to sit down. She was surprised when they listened.

Harper handed Wisdom and Truth to Dayo and told her to ring them and keep chanting. Dayo and Mrs. Nakamura began chanting the binding spell while Harper immediately rang the Bringer harder than she'd ever rung a bell before.

From within the tree, a horrible roar blasted out. The final Razu tore its way out of the tree, nearly splitting it in half. The queen seemed immune to the binding spell, but Harper could see the souls swarming inside the Razu's belly, the spiritual light burning brightly through the monster's pale skin.

The Razu queen first went to the groupings of victims who were still in a deep sleep, but she could not penetrate the salt circle. Kelly had stuffed her hands into her mouth, trying not to scream, but the terror was too obvious not to see. The Razu stood right in front of Kelly, breathing heavily. Harper could see how scared her sister was.

"Don't run, Kelly," Harper urged. "You have to stay in the circle."

The Razu roared, and Kelly screamed. She grabbed her salt container, flipped open the spout, and shook an arc of salt at the monster. The Razu let out a nasty snarl but fell back and returned to Harper's circle, pacing back and forth. The chanting and the ringing of the bells seemed to have no effect on the monster. Suddenly, it found the spot where the Benningtons had broken the salt circle. The creature reached a claw over the broken line of salt, grabbed Olivia by the hair, and tried to pull her out of the circle. Todd held on to his daughter tight.

"No!" Clarissa screamed. She kicked and pummeled the creature, desperately trying to draw it away from her daughter. The Razu let go of Olivia and gouged Clarissa in her abdomen with its claws.

Harper dropped her bells, grabbed the holy water, and raced over to dash it in the Razu's face.

It fell back shrieking, and Harper picked up the Bringer and the Unmaker and began to ring them simultaneously.

"Come to the light and be free," she repeated over and over.

The Razu shook off the effects of the holy water and let out an unholy shriek. It turned toward Harper and bared its sharp fangs.

"Harper, get back into the circle!" Kelly screamed.

Realizing the danger she was in, Harper ran for the salt circle just as the Razu charged. But before it reached her, the free spirits that were flying above them swarmed down and attacked the monster.

"Harper, use the bells now! You can release the souls while it is distracted and losing control."

Harper was stunned to see the ghost of Clarissa now talking to her outside of her physical body.

With a grim nod, Harper rang her bells and called to the spirits within the Razu. Clarissa's spirit joined the others in attacking the monster.

"Come forth, dear ones! Come to the light and be free!" Harper yelled.

Inside the monster's belly the trapped souls were struggling wildly to escape. The spirits pounded relentlessly over and over against the confines of their prison as Harper chanted to them to be free. But it was not enough.

"Why isn't it working?" Dayo shouted.

"I don't know! I think it's too strong!"

"Harper, your grandma said you are really power-ful. You have to channel your powers!"

The Razu roared and lunged at them, chasing Harper back into the salt circle. Mrs. Nakamura lashed at it with her copper wires, backing it away. It was a close call.

"Harper, think about what your grandmother would do," Dayo said. "You can do it."

Harper took a deep breath and focused on the spiritual energy flowing all around her. Grandma Lee said it was concentrated energy that she could harness into a power source. Isn't that what the sha-man did who'd captured the Razu in the first place? But did it mean she would be susceptible to posses-sion? She was scared.

The Razu roared again.

There was no choice.

Closing her eyes, Harper let all her senses open to the spiritual realm. Immediately she was assaulted by the sensation of pure power. It coursed through her body. But it didn't feel anything like a possession. It wasn't an individual spirit. It was just energy. And it only needed direction.

Harper opened her eyes and faced the queen. She dropped her bells, stepped out of the protective salt circle, and walked toward it. The Razu queen moved to attack her. Harper let the pulsing energy course out of her hands and into the belly of the Razu, stopping it midlunge. It twisted in agony as its belly distended and pulsated with the souls frantically trying to escape.

"Oh no you don't!" Harper shouted. "It's time for you to go."

Focusing all her attention on the belly of the queen, Harper felt the flow of the spiritual energy that she'd sent surging into it.

"Bye, now."

Harper exploded the energy within the creature, causing it to erupt from within. All the souls that had been trapped inside the Razu were released in a huge mass of light and joy, which flooded the entire area with happiness.

Holly flew over to Harper, radiant, as she brought two other spirits with her.

"Harper! You did it! You found the light, and you found my parents!"

The ghostly parents smiled at Harper in thanks as they embraced their daughter and flew up to the moonlit path.

"Bye, Harper," Holly said as she disappeared into the sky.

Harper turned around to find everyone kneeling

by the body of Clarissa Bennington. Olivia was weeping uncontrollably as she held her mother's hand.

Next to her, the ghost of Clarissa Bennington appeared.

"Thank you for saving my family and doing the right thing," Clarissa said.

"Thank you for helping me," Harper replied. "But why don't you talk to them before you go?"

Clarissa smiled sadly. "I've done enough harm. I should leave them alone."

Harper shook her head. "No, that would be terrible. Go and talk to them now. Tell your daughter you love her. Tell your husband you forgive him. You shouldn't lose this chance to heal their wounds."

If she could have pushed a ghost, Harper would have. But she was relieved when Clarissa floated over and laid a gentle hand on Olivia's face.

"Mom?" Olivia cried.

Harper turned away to give them privacy and found Dayo and Mrs. Nakamura standing by her, both gazing at the brilliant moonlit path. The rains had stopped, and the sky was a bright star-filled painting.

"It's the most beautiful thing I've ever seen," Dayo said.

Harper did a double take. "You can see them even without touching me?"

Dayo nodded. "I could even see Mrs. Bennington while she was talking to you." With a satisfied breath, Dayo threw her arm around Harper's shoulders. "I guess that makes me a real spirit hunter now, too."

Harper grinned. "Grandma Lee's gonna have to get you your own shaman bells."

"You girls are really amazing," Mrs. Nakamura said. "I think you just saved the entire world. Unfortunately, no one will ever believe it."

"That's okay," Harper said. "We know."

Mrs. Nakamura chuckled.

"Harper!" Kelly was yelling for her.

Kelly was helping Megan stand, the other victims now all awake and staring in shock at the sky above them.

"Do you think they can see the souls also?" Dayo asked.

"Looks like they can," Harper said. "Traumatic experiences change people."

They walked over to Kelly, who threw her arms around the both of them in a tight embrace. "You guys are the coolest, toughest, most amazing middle schoolers in the entire universe."

Harper looked at Kelly curiously. "You okay, Kelly?"

"No, I'm still freaking out," she said. "Why?"

"Because you usually hate this ghost stuff."

Kelly nodded. "Yeah, and I'll probably go back to ignoring it again tomorrow because I hate it. It's too weird. But tonight I'm proud of my little sister and her best friend, who just saved us all."

Kelly's friend Megan approached and swooped in to hug Harper also. "Thank you," she said. "I saw what you did. It felt like a dream, but I know it was real because I can feel the happiness in the air."

She looked up where the spirits danced above them. "They're free at last."

Mrs. Nakamura brought Megan a cup of juice. "Come sit," she said. "This has been very difficult for all of you."

Megan drank the juice gratefully and let Kelly and Mrs. Nakamura seat her next to the others, who were dazed and shocked.

Dayo pulled Harper back to check on the Benningtons. Todd was holding Olivia tight as they both listened to Clarissa's spirit.

"Poor Olivia. She lost one parent and found another," Dayo said.

"Yeah, it makes me appreciate my own parents," Harper said. "Never thought I'd say that."

At that moment, she thought she could hear her father shouting for her. She looked around to see her parents, uncle, and aunt walk into the grove. Uncle Justin and Aunt Caroline immediately ran over to the Benningtons to help them. They didn't see Clarissa's spirit slip silently away toward the light.

Yuna and Peter hurried over to hug Harper and Dayo tight. "Leo told us where you were! We were so worried about you, but we were stuck in the hotel because of the terrible storm!"

At that moment Yuna stared up into the sky and was struck completely dumb. Peter had begun admonishing Harper, when Yuna made him look up. They both stared in complete shock.

Harper stared curiously at them. "Can you see all the spirits?" she asked.

"I can't believe my eyes," Yuna replied.

"Ghosts are real?" Peter asked.

Harper laughed. "Seeing is believing."

"But where are they all going?" Yuna asked.

"Spirits don't belong on earth with us," Harper said with a sad sigh. She thought of her best friend Rose and how much she missed her. "They are going back to where they belong. They're finally free."

She stared up at the night sky, still bright with the free souls that danced across the moonlit path. So many of them. Like a highway of light, they flew overhead.

"Bye, Holly. Bye, Rose."

ALL'S WELL THAT ENDS WELL

Wednesday, November 1

In the morning, Harper's parents were unusually nice and attentive. They'd all stayed up late to explain everything, to everyone, that had happened the night before. Yuna had spent the night hugging them all and crying, while Peter had told Leo's parents about Michael's possession and Harper's past incidents and all that had happened to them since moving to Washington, D.C. Aunt Caroline had been stunned to hear that Leo had also been seeing ghosts, and Uncle Justin just kept shaking his head in disbelief. However, Harper was relieved that for once all the adults believed her. How could they not? They'd all seen the beautiful bridge of souls and heard what the victims had said.

After breakfast, everyone sat together to talk about next steps.

"I couldn't sleep all night. I realized what a horrible daughter I've been to my mom," Yuna said. "When we get home, I'm going to go and talk to her. Really talk. I've been such a fool."

She hugged Harper hard. "I'll never doubt you again."

Harper felt the last vestige of hurt and resentment finally unravel within her.

"Honey, this might be a good time to tell the kids," Peter said to Yuna.

Yuna wiped her eyes and nodded. All the adults looked at each other.

"Kids, so Aunt Caroline and Uncle Justin are going to be taking on even more responsibilities here, with everything that happened," Peter said. "Mr. Bennington and his daughter are coming over soon to discuss what will happen with the hotel. But the one thing that your aunt and uncle have been worried about is Leo's education. So, we've agreed to have Leo live with us during the school year and go to school with you, Harper."

Harper stared aghast at Leo, who glared back at her.

"That's awesome," Dayo said. "Our school is pretty good, for a middle school."

"Cool, Leo," Michael said. "It'll be fun."

"But where will he sleep?" Kelly asked.

"He can have my office," Yuna said. "We'll make it really comfortable for him."

Kelly shrugged and Leo looked unhappy. But it was Harper that everyone seemed to be looking at. She couldn't even roll her eyes or heave a big sigh since they were watching her so closely. What choice did she have? Dayo gave her a little nudge, and Harper immediately smiled.

"That's great," Harper said. "Don't worry, Aunt Caroline and Uncle Justin. Leo will be fine with us."

In the midst of the loud and vocal relief of the parents, the doorbell rang. Todd and Olivia were at the door. As soon as they came in, the adults swept Todd into the office for a private meeting.

While the adults were closeted away and Leo entertained Michael, Harper and Dayo sat with Olivia in their room. Olivia's eyes were swollen from crying.

She sat on Dayo's bed since it was the one that didn't have piles of stuff all over it.

"My dad's really nice," Olivia said with a watery smile. "All these years I thought he didn't care about me, but in fact he cared *too* much. I'm glad he came back, but I miss my mom a lot. And it's hard because I know she did wrong."

Harper and Dayo sat on either side of Olivia to comfort her.

"Everything she did, she did out of love for you," Dayo said.

"She was trying to protect you. Even to the very last moment, all she cared about was saving you," Harper added. "Your mom loved you so much."

Olivia nodded and cried and talked about her mother for a long time. Dayo rubbed her back and Harper kept passing over lots of tissues.

"Well, the good news is that my dad is taking us to New York City because I said I always wanted to live there," Olivia said.

"Oh, me too!" Dayo said.

"Come visit me!" Olivia said. "I'd love to see you both whenever you can."

The girls immediately launched into a discussion of New York, and Harper began to rave about the pizza and bagels and how no other city could ever get them right. Dayo rolled her eyes, causing Olivia to laugh.

"I'm glad I'm leaving the island," Olivia said. "It's too sad here now. All I can think about is my mom."

The friends grew quiet. Dayo gave Olivia a hug while Harper patted her shoulder awkwardly.

"Oh, hey, I'll be able to visit the both of you, too. My dad promised."

Harper beamed happily. "Awesome! You can stay with me. We have lots of room and my house isn't haunted anymore!"

"Or you can stay with me and eat the most amazing food of your life in a house that's never been haunted," Dayo interjected.

Olivia smiled. "Oh no, what do I do?"

Harper frowned. "It's no contest. If I could, I'd live with Dayo also. Her mom's food is seriously the best."

"I tell you what, I'll stay with you first and then we can both go stay with Dayo," Olivia said, throwing her arms around each girl. "That way we'll all be together."

"Brilliant!" Dayo said. "I'll start taking your cookie orders today."

"I'm not sharing mine!" Harper shouted.

Olivia had given Harper and Dayo a bunch of presents to take home. But the gift Harper loved the most was a picture of all three of them on the beach. Olivia had put the photo in a pretty frame decorated with seashells and colorful beads. Harper would treasure it for what it represented: real friends. While she still missed Rose, and always would, it was nice to have two real-life friends.

They were scheduled to take the last shuttle of the day at five p.m. Harper and Dayo were done packing early and were going to look for shells when Yuna appeared and handed Harper the phone. "It's Grandma."

"Grandma!" Harper yelled. "Are you okay? How are you feeling? When are you coming home?"

"I'm fine. Your mom said she'd drive up next week to pick me up. I'd go home now but your aunt Youjin won't let me travel, even though she has a brand-new baby and shouldn't be worrying about me also!"

"Oh, I'll come up, too, Grandma! I have so much to tell you."

"Tell me everything now," Grandma Lee said. "And don't leave anything out."

It took over an hour for Harper to tell the entire story. Dayo chimed in whenever Harper forgot an important point. Grandma was an appreciative audience and asked a lot of questions.

"What happened to Todd and Olivia?" Grandma Lee asked.

"Now that the Razu are gone, they aren't tied

240

to the island anymore," Harper said. "So, Olivia is going to move to New York with her father. They're taking her mother's body to be buried in Florida first. Everything has been hushed up. Olivia said that they had to make payments to everyone to keep quiet about what happened, which I think is just wrong, but I guess that's what really rich people do.

"Oh, but the good news is that Mr. Bennington promoted Aunt Caroline to some top position, and she's now in charge of the whole resort."

"That's wonderful! I always liked your aunt Caroline," Grandma Lee said. "But what about Leo? You still not good with him?"

Harper made a face but was glad her grandmother couldn't see it. "I would have been, but Mom and Dad said that Leo is going to be staying with us for the school year because Aunt Caroline and Uncle Justin are gonna be so busy and they want him to go to school near us. Mom's clearing out her office and turning it into a guest room."

"Maybe he'll be a good help to you," Grandma Lee said, "since he can see spirits also."

"I don't see how," Harper said grudgingly. "He's a big chicken."

"I think hanging around you and Dayo would be good for him."

Harper sighed and looked at her friend, but Dayo just shrugged. "I kind of like him."

"Well, since Leo is going to be living with us, I guess he could train with us," she said grudgingly. "But only if he wants."

"That's my good girl," Grandma Lee said. "Fighting spirits is hard work. The more spirit hunters we have, the safer we all are."

Harper was thinking about this after lunch when Leo pulled her and Dayo aside.

"I just want to thank you for helping me out with the ghost thing," he said.

"Gosh, Leo, it wasn't just for you," Harper snapped.

"I know, I know. You guys are heroes, and I think it is really uncool that the Benningtons are making it all hush-hush. Now no one can know how you saved the world and stuff," Leo said.

Harper's eyes bulged in astonishment. "Leo, did you just compliment me?"

He smiled. "Don't get a big head over it."

"Aw, look at the cousins being so cute and everything," Dayo said.

Both Harper and Leo scowled at her, which made Dayo laugh.

"Look, I just wanted to say I'm sorry about all

those dirty tricks I played on you in the past."

Harper's mouth gaped open again, but this time Dayo nudged her.

"Well, okay then," Harper said. "And thank you."

The cousins smiled at each other. "And if you want, you can learn about being a spirit hunter with me and Dayo."

"Really?" Leo said. "Because I thought about it and realized it would be better to know how to get rid of the bad ones if I ever come across one."

"That would be smart," Harper responded. "So, you're in?"

Leo nodded. "In."

Dayo beamed. "Hey, we'll be like the Three Musketeers, but we'll be the Three Ghostbusteers."

Leo groaned. "That's awful."

"Hey, Dayo can call us whatever she wants as long as she brings her mom's cookies," Harper said.

"You and food." Leo shook his head.

"Should we invite Kelly to join us, too?" Dayo asked.

"No!" Leo and Harper said in unison. The two cousins smiled at each other, finally in complete agreement.

"I think it's going to be fun," Harper said. And she meant it.

ACKNOWLEDGMENTS

If you are here on this page, then that probably means you read this entire book. And that makes you my reader. And that makes me happy. Thank you, dear wonderful reader, for reading my scary little book.